"I'm in love with Daiya."

THE

Empty
AND Box
Zeroth
Maria
6

Kokone Kirino
A girl in the same class as Kazuki. She's cheerful, outgoing, and a bit of a busybody. Daiya Oomine has been a childhood friend of hers since kindergarten, although now he is using a Box in an attempt to rule the world.

EIJI MIKAGE

ILLUSTRATION BY
TETSUO

The Silver Screen of Broken Wishes

A Box that exists solely to destroy
Daiya's Box, "Crime, Punishment,
and the Shadow of Crime."
Launches an assault upon Daiya's
mind in the form of a movie
screening to force him to renounce
his wish.
Once a target is drawn into the
Silver Screen of Broken Wishes,
there is no escape.

Kazuki Hoshino

An extremely ordinary young
man with a decidedly unusual
obsession with maintaining a
normal life. He has become a
favorite object of study for O.
To put a stop to Daiya's
Crime, Punishment, and the
Shadow of Crime, he launches
a counterattack with the Silver
Screen of Broken Wishes.

Daiya Oomine

A cunning cynic with silver hair and earrings. He has no qualms about killing or deceiving if it serves his purposes. Using his Box—Crime, Punishment, and the Shadow of Crime—he faces off against Kazuki.

Crime, Punishment, and the Shadow of Crime

Activates when the target steps on the shadow of its wielder, Daiya. It forces the target to recall the "awareness of sin" in the depths of their heart and places them under Daiya's Rule so that he can control them as he pleases.

Aya Otonashi

A young woman who refers to herself as a "Box" and lives solely to grant the wishes of others. Rejecting her attachment to Kazuki, she has discarded the name Maria and has decided to live as Aya.

"What?"

"I said, just kidding, Oomine. Please don't be angry. It's not what you think. I'm actually helping you."

"You're trying to say that leaking my plans is helping me?"

"That's right."

"Maybe this is what you're getting at. You did this..."

"...to draw Kazuki into the Silver Screen of Broken Wishes."

"Exactly. Don't you think that's the most reliable way of getting him to do what you want? Hey, Otonashi. It'll bring Kazuki here, right?"

"...Yeah, it almost certainly will."

"See? I have helped you."

I turn my unfocused gaze to concentrate on a single point.

"Haven't seen you in a while."

Kazuki Hoshino is there.

Straining against the sluggishness of the Silver Screen of Broken Wishes, I get to my feet.

"Yeah. I feel that way, too," Kazu replies with a weak smile.

A plain plastic case is dangling from his hand.

That's why I'm even more interested in the state of his right hand and the weapon it holds than I am in the case.

"Kazu, what's up with your hand?"

It's wrapped in bandages. They're stained with blood, suggesting the injury happened just recently.

"…This is my line in the sand."

He takes a step forward.
Kazuki Hoshino and I stand confronting each other.

Yeah—
Not a shred of doubt about it.
My face-off with Kazu began in the Game of Indolence, and now it ends here.

"I remembered I gave up on you."

Kasumi Mogi
A girl who continues to live her life optimistically despite meeting with an accident. Once the object of Kazuki's one-sided affections, she came to harbor similar feelings for him, but now...

Designed by Toru Suzuki

THE Empty Box AND Zeroth Maria

6

EIJI MIKAGE

ILLUSTRATION BY TETSUO

New York

The Empty Box and Zeroth Maria, Vol. 6
Eiji Mikage

Translation by Luke Baker
Cover art by Tetsuo

UTSURO NO HAKO TO ZERO NO MARIA Vol. 6
©EIJI MIKAGE 2013
First published in Japan in 2013 by KADOKAWA CORPORATION, Tokyo.
English translation rights arranged with KADOKAWA CORPORATION, Tokyo,
through TUTTLE-MORI AGENCY, INC., Tokyo.

English translation © 2019 by Yen Press, LLC

Yen On
1290 Avenue of the Americas
New York, NY 10104

Visit us at yenpress.com
facebook.com/yenpress
twitter.com/yenpress
yenpress.tumblr.com
instagram.com/yenpress

First Yen On Edition: June 2019

Yen On is an imprint of Yen Press, LLC.
The Yen On name and logo are trademarks of Yen Press, LLC.

Library of Congress Cataloging-in-Publication Data
Names: Mikage, Eiji author. | 415, illustrator. |
Tetsuo (Illustrator), illustrator. | Baker, Luke, translator.
Title: The empty box and zeroth Maria / Eiji Mikage ; illustration by 415,
Tetsuo ; translation by Luke Baker.
Other titles: Utsuro no Hako to Zero no Maria. English
Description: New York, NY : Yen On, 2017– | v. 1 illustration by 415 — vols. 2–7
illustration by Tetsuo.
Identifiers: LCCN 2017027929 | ISBN 9780316561105 (v. 1 : paperback) |
ISBN 9780316561112 (v. 2 : paperback) | ISBN 9780316561136 (v. 3 : paperback) |
ISBN 9780316561143 (v. 4 : paperback) | ISBN 9780316561174 (v. 5 : paperback) |
ISBN 9780316561198 (v. 6 : paperback)
Subjects: CYAC: Science fiction. | BISAC: FICTION / Science Fiction / General.
Classification: LCC PZ7.1.M553 Em 2017 | DDC [Fic]—dc23
LC record available at https://lccn.loc.gov/2017027929

ISBNs: 978-0-316-56119-8 (paperback)
978-0-316-56120-4 (ebook)

1 3 5 7 9 10 8 6 4 2

LSC-C

Printed in the United States of America

◆◆◆ Daiya Oomine 09/11 FRI 10:00 PM ◆◆◆

Aya Otonashi, the older sister of Maria Otonashi, is dead. At least, according to the family registry.

I learned about this before I was pulled into the Game of Indolence. I had been investigating Otonashi, hoping to find some clue on how to better use my Box.

Maria Otonashi.

She was the second daughter born to Michishige Otonashi, an executive at a major finance company. She belonged to a family of four—her father, Michishige; her mother, Yukari; an older sister, Aya; and Maria herself—who lived in a house in an upper-class neighborhood of Hamako Prefecture. Maria's parents were quite a few years apart in age, with her father nearing a ripe sixty around the time she was fourteen, whereas her mother was still only thirty-five. It also turned out that Michishige had married three times, with Yukari being his third wife.

I can imagine that that alone would make for some complicated family relationships, but Maria's relationship with Aya was especially so.

The two sisters had different mothers. The one who gave birth to Aya wasn't Yukari but rather Michishige's previous wife. What's more, big sister Aya was still only three months older than Maria, so they were also in the same year of school.

That being the case, Michishige had Aya and Maria attend different elementary and middle schools to avoid causing a stir among their classmates.

The two were apparently polar opposites.

Aya, the elder sister, was a student who stood out at every turn. She was one of the best in her class in both study and athletics, and she was always the center of attention. Aya was entrusted with important roles like student council president almost as a matter of course, and there wasn't a student in her school who didn't know her name.

On the other hand, her younger sister, Maria, was a reserved and inconspicuous student. She was often picked on in elementary school, perhaps because she never fought back. This was probably why she frequently stayed home from school, claiming to have a headache or stomachache, and even when she did go, she would be holed up in the school infirmary instead of participating. Word has it her grades weren't all that great, either, but I think that almost goes without saying.

But the one who proved to be a problem child for her teachers wasn't Maria, the poor student who disliked going to school and kept to herself. Aya was a model pupil on the surface, but she was a handful.

When you are trying to guide a student, trouble can occur when she excels too much—all the more so when the student understands the situation and goes out of her way to show off her abilities rather than downplaying them.

Aya was more knowledgeable about each subject than her instructors and wouldn't hesitate to point out any mistake they made. She would resolve incidents of bullying by suggesting a more effective method than those of her teachers. When an argument arose, Aya would shoot down the adults who were supposed to be the peacekeepers.

Thanks to all of this, it became evident that Aya's teachers were not as smart as she was. It was so obvious, even the other students could tell.

Students don't respect teachers who aren't as intelligent as they are. Because of Aya, the teachers lost their authority as grown-ups, and any class with her in it was consistently unruly because no one would obey the instructor. It wasn't a typical sort of unruliness, either, but something deeper and more unsettling. This much was plain from the severity of the problems that occurred.

For example, you could look at the injuries and attempted suicides in the classes to which Aya belonged.

There were also three teachers who quit after interacting with her. One began suffering mental illness, one became violent with a student and injured them, and one became so obsessed with his pupil Aya that he began borderline stalking her.

All the same, despite their different mothers and opposite symmetry, Aya and Maria were by all accounts on very good terms.

They apparently called each other regularly during breaks at school, and on days off, they were seen hanging out together hand in hand. A classmate of Aya's, who had been around the two of them while they were together, had this to say:

"They were super-close. They looked totally different from friends or sisters... Maybe twins? That's not quite it, either. I guess the closest thing would be...like they were lovers."

As far as I could find, there wasn't anything grave about their relationship. Considering the convoluted state of their family, they didn't have any major problems at home, either. Aya's mother had gotten a divorce because of Maria's birth, but they had no real trouble with her, since they had been sure to make solid financial arrangements. Their father, Michishige, was well aware that their family was not normal and thus kept a watchful eye over the household.

Of course, these are answers I was able to find just by asking around. I won't know the truth of things like what actually went on within the family unless I dig much deeper. But I'm confident in saying there wasn't any familial breakdown that would have been readily apparent to someone on the outside, as in the case of Ryu Miyazaki and Riko Asami.

All the same, there is no denying that this family no longer exists.

In the end, the other three members aside from Maria met their untimely deaths in a car accident.

I don't know much about the wreck. It was a head-on collision between two passenger vehicles, but the other driver is dead, and without any witnesses, no one knows the details of the incident.

Regardless, the rest of the family aside from Maria, who was at home alone, was killed. That is an incontrovertible fact.

Maria Otonashi was all on her own. As someone who struggled to open herself to anyone but her family, Maria Otonashi was utterly and truly alone.

After she received her inheritance and Michishige's younger brother Kiyohiko became her legal guardian, Maria disappeared.

That's pretty much everything I was able to dig up about Maria Otonashi.

I have no idea how Maria Otonashi came across the miracle of the Boxes. I also don't know why she wanted to become someone who made wishes come true, or how she got ahold of the Misbegotten Happiness.

Nevertheless, there's no way the loss of her family didn't have some connection. The deaths of her loved ones drove Maria mad, planting the seeds of her abnormally self-sacrificing mentality. That in turn created the aloof and detached girl we know today.

What's more, she was presented with an opportunity that would lead her to perfect this persona. Within the repeating world of the Rejecting Classroom, Maria had an entire life's worth of time at her disposal. Maybe Maria believed that if she could become Aya, her all-too-perfect older sister, her wish would be granted. And indeed, she did transform in her attempt to assume Aya's identity.

Yeah. I had all that figured out, so I suppose I should have discovered O's true nature much sooner.

…Well, to be honest, I shouldn't have discovered it at all. I was never meant to connect O with something so mundane as her family.

The thing about enigmas is that the more you understand them, the less enigmatic they become. You'll never be able to use a Box to the fullest unless you keep it at arm's length, accept it blindly, and give up on trying to comprehend it. For something inexplicable, you should never seek out any meaning beyond its inherent mystery.

But I despise that kind of unconditional acceptance. For me, it's the most difficult thing to do.

Yep, it was as simple as that. Shutting off my brain ran contrary to my wish, so there's no way I could do it.

That's why I created limitations for my Box that left me unable to wield it properly. I suppose I should think about the trade-off: I was able to make Crime, Punishment, and the Shadow of Crime realistic for me.

At any rate, it was only a matter of time before I pieced together O's true nature.

In a twist that's almost too simple, the name O is just the initial for "Otonashi." And considering how Maria started going by her older sister's name, I'm sure I've interpreted things correctly.

O's name is—

—Aya Otonashi.

Otonashi, Yuri Yanagi, and I are within the Silver Screen of Broken Wishes, just as before.

The Box takes the form of a red movie theater.

The impossible, unreal cleanliness of this place is putting me under slowly increasing pressure, as if it's trying to eliminate my human filth. It's an ongoing attack meant to wear down my mind and put an end to my wish.

Amid this pressure, I ponder something that has been bothering me.

This is strange.

I look around.

The curved passage covered in immaculate red carpet connects to four theaters.

On the electric sign hanging in the middle of the lobby we are currently in is written the message THE SCREENING OF *REPEAT, RESET, RESET* HAS ENDED.

I've been forced to watch three movies so far:

Breaking of Close Ties,

A 60.5-Foot Gulf, and

Repeat, Reset, Reset.

They presented my past from the perspectives of Miyuki Karino, Haruaki Usui, and Maria Otonashi, respectively. Expertly edited to make me suffer, these films were an attack, a screening of my sins. There are four theaters, which means there's one more movie left.

Its title is *15 Years Old and Earrings*, running from ten thirty PM to midnight. If I don't resolve this today, my defeat is certain.

But this is strange.

I thought I had already taken care of Kazu.

"Oomine, what's with that look?" someone asks as I scowl.

…No, I probably shouldn't call this girl "Maria" now that she's done away with her demure past self.

"Aya, I have a question." I use her other name instead, and oddly enough, it feels right.

Yeah, I guess that's how it should feel. When we first met within the Rejecting Classroom, "Aya Otonashi" was her only name. The girl with me now is the Aya Otonashi she built to pursue her ideals over the decades in that time loop.

I couldn't have called her Maria while the world was still on repeat. That name was one she said purely on a lark, a false name that should have been lost to oblivion. "Maria Otonashi" never existed in that world, and Aya never intended for her to, either.

That she did was a miracle only Kazu could have brought about, as someone who was able to retain his memories in that world.

You could say Kazu threw a monkey wrench into Aya Otonashi's plans, changing her fate.

I, on the other hand, was no miracle worker. It was impossible for me to hold on to the name Maria through the repetitions.

For me, she has always been "Aya Otonashi," even if she originally borrowed the name from her older sister.

With no particular reaction to my calling her Aya, she asks, "What's your question?"

I tell her about the discrepancy. "Why hasn't the Silver Screen of Broken Wishes ended?"

Aya frowns. "What're you talking about? That's simple. It just means Kazuki Hoshino hasn't destroyed the Silver Screen of Broken Wishes."

"But don't you see what I'm getting at? *Why* hasn't Kazu done that? He should have been heartbroken the moment you stopped being Maria Otonashi. He would have given up the fight almost as a matter of course, don't you think? Why is the Silver Screen of Broken Wishes still around?"

Yes, this fight should have been settled.

After all, Aya Otonashi is here. Kazu should be in total despair.

Why hasn't this ended? Why hasn't his heart been broken?

"Oomine, you're completely clueless. Somehow, you don't understand just how terrifying Kazuki Hoshino is."

"What do you mean?"

Aya replies without a change in expression. "It's easy. His heart isn't broken."

"What?"

That doesn't make sense.

Kazu's mission is to bring Maria Otonashi a normal life, free of the Boxes. But he would have seen the futility of his endeavor the moment she arrived here in the Silver Screen of Broken Wishes and decided to erase "Maria Otonashi." It's no longer possible. Surely he must feel it even more acutely than I do.

So why is his heart still intact?

"Are you suggesting that Kazu still thinks there's something he can do for you?"

"Exactly. He's not normal. He will never give up, as long as his purpose has not vanished. He could have zero chance of achieving it, but it wouldn't matter. I believe the very idea of throwing in the towel has never even existed for him."

He has no concept of giving up...?

That's not possible. And yet, the truth is that the Silver Screen of Broken Wishes is still in effect. Plus, I can't imagine Aya being mistaken about Kazu's nature.

Meaning it's the truth.

Which means...

"...This is bad."

From the beginning, this battle has been about breaking Kazu's heart. With Aya as she is now, he has no chance of completing his mission. He has failed for certain. However he wants to think about it, I can't see it any other way.

But just because Kazu has lost doesn't mean I've won. At this rate, it's going to be a loss for both of us. If Kazu isn't broken and the Silver Screen of Broken Wishes doesn't come to a halt, then the fourth movie, *15 Years Old and Earrings*, will be shown. Once it ends, my Box will be destroyed, regardless of whether I want it to or not. If that happens, then it goes without saying that my plans to use Crime, Punishment, and the Shadow of Crime to mass-produce dog-people and heighten people's individual sense of ethics will go up in a puff of smoke.

As things stand now, I'm going to lose, too.

Why is this happening? This was going according to plan. I neutralized Yuri Yanagi right away when she was sent in here as an assassin, and I successfully summoned Aya here to me. Nevertheless, I don't have any more cards to play. I haven't failed, yet I'm on the brink of defeat... What the hell is with that guy? Is he like some boxer who's immune to punches?

Now I see why O thinks I don't stand a chance against him.

"Otonashi." Yuri Yanagi finally speaks.

I listen closely, thinking whatever she says could lead to a breakthrough.

"You used to call him by just his first name, but now you've stopped."

But it's just the most meaningless crap ever.

It pisses me off.

"What the hell, bitch? You wanna know now that they've split up? You think it's your big chance to hook up with Kazu? You're a real pain in the ass, so just keep your mouth shut, you stupid slut!"

"Whooooa! Where do you get off talking like that?! You're awful! You've been acting like I'm not even here this entire time, too!"

"That's what you do with the characters who've played out their role. Aya has been at odds with Kazu all along, so you're worthless now. You're worthless in this story, and yet you insist on ruining the pacing with your babbling, you empty-eyed *teru teru bozu* doll. Go pray for fair weather somewhere else."

"S-so I'm getting in the way just by talking?!"

There's no bigger waste of time than dealing with her, so I ignore her retort.

But it is true that Aya has changed how she refers to Kazu. Maybe she can't be so familiar now that she considers him an enemy.

An enemy.

An enemy, huh...?

"By the way, Aya, I'm just checking, but can I assume this means you're on my side now? Kazu's going to keep hounding you until he breaks, right? You need to see him lose."

"Yes, I do need him beaten. Kazuki Hoshino is not someone I can afford to ignore. There's probably no way of fighting him, but that doesn't mean I can lower my guard. I still see him as the greatest obstacle to my goals."

"I suppose you're right. Working with me for the time being is your best option in my mind, so how about it?"

Aya is silent for a moment. "...I can't accept your Box," she says, "your Crime, Punishment, and the Shadow of Crime. The way you sacrifice others goes against my principles. You and I are alike, yes, but I cannot accept your methods."

"...So you're saying you won't join forces with me?"

If not, there's no way forward for me. Kazu still hasn't given up the fight, even under these circumstances. No matter how you slice it, if I'm going to break Kazu, then getting Aya involved is a must.

"No. I'll help you."

That's why her reply inevitably puts my mind at ease.

"There's no doubt that crushing him comes before anything else. I just want to say, though, that I am only working toward my own ends, not trying to save you. For example, you may have a time limit, but I don't. The difference may not work in your favor."

"Same goes for me. I may betray you depending on how things go."

"Then I don't see a problem."

"Great. So let me ask you something. I'm not clear on how to break Kazu. But you know, don't you, Aya? Tell me. What's the most effective way for me to attack Kazu?"

"......"

Aya falls silent.

There are two reasons why I asked this question. The first is simple. Aya understands Kazu inside and out, so she can concoct a better means of getting at him than I can.

The other is to confirm that Aya really has severed her attachments to Kazu.

It may not show on the surface, but with their relationship being what it was, I wouldn't be surprised if she still had some feelings for him. The last threads of her bond with Kazu could even lead her to put forth weak ideas. In that case, she would become a hindrance. The best thing to do would be to get as much use out of her as I can but keep her at a distance.

But Aya's answer is:

"I need to forget about Kazuki Hoshino."

Not even a shred of affection for him left. It's obvious in her reply.

"If I use the Misbegotten Happiness on someone he knows, then I'll forget all about him. It'll be like what we built in the world of repetition never existed. That's what I need to do."

Her idea—

Her idea is guaranteed to succeed.

Kazu still holds on to hope without breaking because he knows he is special to Aya. Put another way, it's *all* he has.

Without that, his last hope would be gone.

So he needs to become a stranger to her. Someone who isn't special to her in the slightest.

Still—

"……You…"

My hands are trembling at what Aya has just said. I mean, how can she say such a thing so calmly?

The two of them cared for each other. It was a powerful interdependence. A firm bond. A connection so profound that without it, the two of them would become completely different people.

And now Aya Otonashi is saying she's going to just throw it away.

"Are you really okay with that?" I ask without thinking, but I already know the answer.

She is. She could never mention a plan like this if she weren't. Aya must be some superhuman, her emotions immune even to forgetting about Kazu. A monster on some level I can't fathom.

But instead, she says:

"I'm not."

"...What?"

My thoughts screech to a halt.

That was completely unexpected. Much, much more unexpected than a stony, superhuman declaration that she didn't mind at all.

"Of course I can't be okay with it. If I were, I never would have done what I did to stay with Kazuki Hoshino all this time. If I refuse to admit he was important to me, I'd just be running away. There's no way I can face him if I don't accept this."

It will be painful to forget Kazuki Hoshino, Aya is saying clearly.

I don't understand.

"Then—"

Why is she able to suggest such a thing?

Why is she able to suggest an idea where the biggest sacrifice is her own feelings?

"But what he is to me is not an issue."

"...Why?!"

"Because my feelings will not interfere whatsoever."

"____"

My breath catches in my throat. Aya said it without the slightest hint of doubt.

"If I feel anything in conflict with my mission, I'll ignore it. I am not so weak-minded as that. Nothing within me can shake my own resolve."

I know when I see how distant she is. I know when I see that she is so detached from her own emotions that they hardly seem to be her own.

She's telling the truth.

"I'm not human. I exist solely to grant the wishes of others—I am a Box."

She's speaking figuratively, of course. Aya is a human with a body—but this is the level of her resolve to live the life she does.

And that's exactly what she's doing.

Aya will not accept any other meaning to her life aside from fulfilling her purpose. She will never allow herself to get in the way of her goal. The same goes for those important to her, and even her own death.

She's a machine. An effigy. An aberration. A Box.

I strive to be the same.

That's how I've tried to create my ideal world.

But seeing how successfully she's removed herself from humanity, can I really say I would be capable of the same?

"..
...."

—No way.

I could understand if she had said yes, forgetting Kazu wouldn't bother her. If numbing my heart was all it took, then I think I might still have it in me, too.

This is different, though. Aya Otonashi is capable of achieving her ends without forsaking her normal emotions.

I can't do that.

It's impossible.

When it comes down to it, I'm human.

In fact, I—

"Ngh."

The instant I think this, the shadows of crime within me go berserk.

Yes. In fact, the pain of these shadows of crime, which I myself created, may already be too much for me.

The shadows of crime I brought into myself in order to Rule will rage within me if I give them an opening. It's gradually growing worse.

I clench my teeth. *Agh, dammit, it's like cannonballs shooting through my veins. Why is so much pain bubbling up within me? And this is just the suffering I've created for myself.*

Why am I so mediocre?

Why am I just some nobody who can't even cause a miracle?

I touch my earrings. I want to change. I don't want to be that stupid, naive boy again. I want to continue struggling against this horrible world. But...

But...

But the truth is—

Light. Darkness. The sea. The world. A business hotel. The womb. Hands clasped together. A crying face. A shutout victory. The world. Body heat. Cold. Cold. The tingling of a left hand through a catcher's mitt. Differences in ability. Envy. Dreams. Confessions. Checking someone's mood. Cigarettes. Bruises. Trembling hands. Fear. Hatred. Hatred. Hatred. Hatred. Hatred. Hatred. Crime. Punishment. Justice. Crime for the sake of justice. Earrings.

My breath still ragged, I touch my earrings one more time.

When did I get these piercings again?

As I ponder this, the one I hate more than anyone else forces their way into my head. Miyuki Karino.

Rino was incapable of reflecting on her actions. She had no sense that she had done anything wrong. I had no choice but to make her understand; I wouldn't feel right until I made sure she knew the full weight of what she'd done to Kiri. Otherwise, I wouldn't have been able to stand the injustice of the world. So I gave her what she deserved. I refused to forgive Rino until I heard her express her sincere regret. All she could do was offer an empty "I'm sorry." That's why I never forgave her, nor had any reason to do so. *"Please tell me what I need to do,"* she had said. *Why can't you think of that on your own? "I love you. I did it because I've always loved you,"* she'd said. *Shut the hell up. Are you trying to flatter me or something? No, that's not it. She's saying it's all my fault. You're letting me know that it was my existence that hurt Kiri, aren't you, you piece of shit?* Before I knew it, I was hitting Rino. I couldn't believe what I was doing. It didn't seem real, turning violent toward someone I'd known since childhood. It distanced me from my reality. While my body registered the physical impact, the sensation was removed from me, as if it were happening to someone else. The person battering Rino wasn't me. It was someone else within me, whom I could no longer control. *"I'm sorry, I'm sorry, I'm sorry."* Don't be stupid. *That's not how you beg forgiveness from someone who's hurting you!*

It didn't resolve anything.

It didn't resolve *anything.*

There was no way *to* resolve it.

Without a Box, I was truly powerless.

I knew. I knew what had happened to Rino in the hotel. I knew she had feelings for me. I even knew all the best things about her, like how she was cheerful and easy to talk to, how she was so openhearted with others, how she could be happy when it was time to be happy and sad when it was time to be sad. I knew she wasn't a bad person. But I couldn't forgive her. I couldn't. I just couldn't.

That created the discord inside me. I shouldn't have hit Rino, but I also had no other choice. So I split up my image of Rino and erased the part of her that caused me trouble. I forgot she was my old friend.

That was how I condemned her.

I dyed my hair. I pierced my ears. I longed to forsake the "Daiya Oomine" I once was and become someone else. If my affable nature was what had led Kiri to such a fate, then I would do away with that version of me.

I know; you don't need to tell me.

I'm no superhuman.

I can never be an "Aya Otonashi."

The only difference between me and everyone else is that I can look at myself from a distance. That's enough for me.

—That's enough for me.

I finally fight down the shadows of crime and regain control of myself.

"Is something wrong, Oomine?"

"A-are you all right?"

Aya and Yanagi are talking to me.

"......It's nothing."

...What the hell am I getting so upset about?

Yeah, some parts of me are still weak. No need to dwell on it.

If my emotions are going to sway me, then I'll just have to avert my eyes and ignore them. I don't have to take them head-on like Aya. I pieced that together long ago, which is why I've been doing it all along. It's why I've been able to cut off my emotions in favor of logic. That's my weapon. I should be proud of my abilities.

"Aya," I say, now that I've collected myself, "going back to what we were talking about earlier. I agree that we should use your Misbegotten Happiness to take down Kazu. Have you already worked out the details?"

"No, not yet. I only just came up with the idea now, after all."

That makes sense. Scheming is surprisingly difficult for Aya Otonashi. Those squeaky-clean values of hers prevent her from adopting an underhanded approach. Yep, even Aya has weaknesses. There's no use comparing my abilities with hers.

"Oomine, what do you think?"

"Losing your memories is pretty much guaranteed to get good results. But even if you do erase your memory, it'll be pointless if we don't let Kazu know about it, right?"

"Won't he find out on his own, even if we don't go to the trouble of telling him?"

"That may work for you, but I don't have time. I have to show Kazu that you don't even remember him."

"Hmm, I suppose you're right. And that means—"

"Yeah. I need you to use the Misbegotten Happiness right in front of him."

"I can enter Boxes, but I can't escape them. If I'm here, then Kazuki Hoshino—"

"I'll call him into the Silver Screen of Broken Wishes."

That is the first prerequisite for breaking his spirit.

"What will it take to get him to come here, though?" she asks. "From where he stands, it's better to destroy your Box from a safe distance. All he has to do is wait for barely two hours. I can't imagine him taking the risk of coming here, you know?"

"I can take care of that if I use Crime, Punishment, and the Shadow of Crime."

"Then who should I use the Misbegotten Happiness on?"

"That depends on what Kazu does, but as of right now, there are three of us in here. Which means the best candidate has already been decided."

I shift my gaze to Yanagi.

"Huh?"

"Lucky you, Yuri Yanagi. There was a brief period when you had no reason to be here, but now you get a new role."

"Um? Um? Oh..."

Yanagi's face goes pale as she catches my drift.

Seeing this, Aya steps in front of Yanagi as if to protect her.

"...Sorry, but I have no intention of using my Misbegotten Happiness on anyone who doesn't want help. Not even to defeat Kazuki Hoshino."

So that's how it is. I guess that part of her won't change even when her resolve is this strong. She's still unable to sacrifice another, no matter how inefficient it makes her plans.

...No, that isn't surprising, in a sense. If she weren't like that, it would go against her personal mission of making others happy.

"I see. Well then, I guess we'll have to find someone else for the job." I immediately realize I won't break her on this, so I offer a perfunctory comment to bring us to a temporary resolution.

Aya gives a small nod of understanding.

Truthfully, I hold Yanagi's shadow of a crime within me, so I can make her beg for salvation just like that. She was hurt badly by the Game of Indolence; if I dig at those wounds, Yanagi will probably be quick to ask for deliverance. Her sins are weightier than the average person's, after all.

Of course, there's no need to fixate solely on Yanagi. If all we're doing is erasing Aya's memories of Kazu, then we can use anyone who knows him, no problem.

However, I can't place my hopes on an uncertain third party when I don't know if they will come or not. If I want a guaranteed sacrifice, it would seem I really do need Yanagi.

Once I've thought about this, I return to the conversation.

"I'll summon Kazu into the Silver Screen of Broken Wishes by the end of the fourth movie, *15 Years Old and Earrings*. Then we'll use your Misbegotten Happiness on someone he knows, right in front of him. If that part's set in stone, then I guess the issue is how."

"Right. You say it's going to work out somehow, but how do you plan to pull it off?"

"Let's see…"

How about I threaten to kill Aya if he doesn't call off the Silver Screen of Broken Wishes? The question is whether that would actually persuade him, but chances are high that Kazu would play along for Aya's sake even if he doubted the threat itself.

So should I relay the message to him using Crime, Punishment, and the Shadow of Crime? I'd love it if I could tell him without any trouble, but it could prove surprisingly difficult to convey it to him reliably in the short time I have left. Damn, if only O would help me, I could be sure he would know—

Do you have a wish?

—No, hold on. I'm forgetting something huge, aren't I? How did Kazu get ahold of the Silver Screen of Broken Wishes in the first place?

It goes without saying. He got O to give it to him. Kazu went to O for help in order to defeat me.

O is on his side, not mine.

So we know O has already given Kazu a Box. As long as the two of them aren't at odds in some way I don't know about, I have to keep in mind that O might come to Kazu's aid.

Just now, I considered threatening to kill Aya, so let's say I go through with it. Even if I do succeed in delivering the message to Kazu, can I be sure O won't screw me over by giving him more information—telling him the threat is a bluff, perhaps? Can I rule that out?

Of course not. It's more than possible. In that case, I have no choice but to outwit O as well.

O isn't perfect, but it seems she can see what goes on in the world. There's a chance she might overhear if I go blabbing my strategy to Aya. However, O can't read minds. If I keep quiet, I should be able to keep my intentions hidden from her. Just like with a human.

In short, I'll conceal my real plans from Aya, trick O into thinking the plot puts Kazu at an advantage, and then get Kazu to come to the Silver Screen of Broken Wishes of his own volition. That's what it comes down to.

...*What the hell? That's way too hard.*

"Oomine, you've gone quiet. Does that mean you can't come up with anything?"

I peer into Aya's face.

It's blank.

Her emotions are perfectly repressed.

I suddenly recall a few lines from *Repeat, Reset, Reset*.

"I know what results from asking a Box for such a wish. The outcome is—

"—ruin.

"But then what will I do if you learn of the Boxes anyway and obtain one? I won't feel inspired to steal it from you. I may not stand against you, like I would against other owners.

"We will be partners again— No, we won't. I won't work with you. I don't want to interfere with your affairs, either. I guess we'll both just be moving in the same direction. We were never meant to be partners. Our original relationship—

"—was as kindred spirits."

"......I almost miss it," I whisper without thinking.

What's that supposed to mean? I wonder a second later.

What she said to me in the movie—in that reset—pops into my head and then really sticks with me.

—Just what is "Aya Otonashi" to me?

For Kazu, "Aya Otonashi" is the enemy. Kazu wants to make Aya—no, in this situation it's more correct to say "Maria"—a part of his normal life. That's why "Aya Otonashi," the self-proclaimed Box trying to relinquish her humanity, is his greatest obstacle.

But for me, it's the opposite: "Maria Otonashi" poses the problem for me.

"......"

Problem?

Why?

Will it be troublesome because Aya and I have similar goals? Because we're working together? Because she was once my partner even in the Rejecting Classroom? ...I get the feeling it's something different. None of these fit the bill.

I need her on a much deeper level.

So it must have something to do with my mission.

I think it's fine if I'm not the one to see this mission through. In the near future, I will collapse under the weight of my sins. When I do, my mission will most likely still be incomplete. I'm okay with that as long as there is someone like Shindo to carry on my will so that the world does eventually change. I don't care if I'm cast aside like garbage or despised. I don't even care if I die.

So—

Yeah...I've got it. I've figured out what Aya Otonashi is to me.

Aya Otonashi is my hope.

She wishes for a world where everyone is happy. If that becomes reality, my purpose will be achieved at the same time. When her wish comes true, so does mine.

And seeing her gives me hope that her wish, a far more difficult wish than mine, might very well become reality.

Her detachment.

Her nobility.

Her righteousness.

Her honesty.

They will save even my wish.

No, it's not just me.

They will save every owner. She is hope to all of us.

That's why she has taken O's name. She will grant the wishes of everyone.

She is a hallowed entity who must be protected at all costs.

That's why I cannot forgive him.

I cannot forgive Kazuki Hoshino for trying to stamp down our wishes for the sake of his trite goal—his selfish desire—to be with "Maria."

We have to shatter Kazu utterly.

"I did come up with one plan."

To that end, I will deceive Aya and O and everyone else so that I can plunge Kazu into despair.

"Maybe we should use Kasumi Mogi."

Kazu.

I will never let you take back the zeroth Maria.

◇◇◇ Kazuki Hoshino 09/11 FRI 10:03 PM ◇◇◇

What's the best way to describe this sensation?

Nothing has changed about me, yet I'm clearly different from before.

All I've really done is come to understand myself. As if I had read my own user's manual. That was enough to alter this world, though. A strange feeling is running through me and leaving me refreshed, as if someone has injected menthol into my blood. My thoughts are growing more and more organized as things fall into place.

The fog hanging over the world is lifting.

It's getting clearer.

And clearer.

The world opens up before me.

Now I can focus solely on helping Maria.

Now that I have the Empty Box, I'm transformed.

"Whoa, what happened to her?"

That's the first thing out of Haruaki's mouth when he reaches the tunnel beneath the elevated tracks, by the embankment outside of downtown. His face is as white as a sheet. He's looking at Iroha, who's still unconscious and sitting against the wall covered with graffiti so bad it doesn't even qualify as street art.

"H-hey, Hosshi, don't tell me you killed her or something?"

"She's alive."

"M-man, what's with all that blood...?"

True, there is red liquid on the ground and wall. On Iroha's face and clothes as well.

"It's fake."

"F-fake blood? Really?"

Haruaki squats down and touches the red liquid on the ground, then sniffs it on his hand. After grimacing for a moment, he nods slightly several times in agreement that the blood is indeed fake.

"I-it definitely isn't blood. Still, what's up with all this? Why is she out cold?"

Haruaki peers into Iroha's face, then checks her pulse and breathing. Her face is illuminated by the lantern, but I can't see it from my position.

What did I do to Iroha? Explaining could take a while, so I settle for answering the first half of his questions about how things ended up this way.

"Daiya and Iroha came up with a scheme to show Maria I betrayed her. I completely fell for it, and now Maria is inside the Silver Screen of Broken Wishes."

"Which means she must have found out about Daiya's Box, huh?"

"Yeah."

Haruaki knows the situation is grave. He scowls, stands up, and gives me a hard look. "Why didn't you call me before that happened? Don't you think you can count on me?"

It comes across almost as a threat. As tall as Haruaki is, I can certainly feel his intensity.

"You've got it wrong. I couldn't call you because they warned me to come alone," I insist, but then I realize that wasn't the only reason. "...Actually, I wouldn't have been able to call you even if they hadn't."

"Then why?!" Haruaki yells. He's upset he wasn't able to help me.

I'm incredibly fortunate.

And I'm reassured.

I'm truly happy I became friends with Haruaki.

"It's the opposite. The truth is, I didn't call you because I do count on you."

"Huh?"

"I count on you so much, it feels like I'm completely dependent..."

If not, I would never have gotten him involved in this. I wouldn't have to keep beating myself up for teaching him about Boxes.

"...I-if you're counting on me, then why?"

"You were with Kokone, right? I wanted you to keep her safe. Do you understand why?"

"Oh..." Haruaki scratches his cheek with his finger to hide his embarrassment. "That makes sense... We thought Daiyan was going after Kiri."

"Yeah. Even if he hadn't threatened me, we would have thought this whole situation was just Daiya's attempt at a diversion."

Yep, I had believed that Daiya was gunning for Kokone, that she was in greater danger than Maria or I was. And I had good reason to.

After all, I'd assumed Daiya would have figured out by then that I wasn't the owner of the Silver Screen of Broken Wishes.

If he did know, then he would try to do something about the real owner before he went for me or Maria. Obviously, he would go after Kokone before Maria.

But he didn't.

"So Daiya really hasn't put two and two together about the owner?"

"Seems that way."

The Silver Screen of Broken Wishes is a Box that exists solely to eliminate Daiya's. He should have picked up on it the moment Yuri entered the Silver Screen of Broken Wishes and the screens continued to show only Daiya's past.

How does he still not realize I'm not the owner?

I might *have* a Box, sure. If worse came to worst, sure—I would want to contact O, get ahold of a Box, and take down Daiya. It would definitely be my last resort, but I have thought about it.

But even if I had gotten a Box, I wouldn't have wished for this. My Box would never have ended up like the Silver Screen of Broken Wishes. I could never create a Box meant entirely to save Daiya alone.

I mean, it would be impossible for anyone who wasn't thinking only of Daiya from the bottom of their heart.

It would be impossible for anyone unless they only had eyes for Daiya—unless they were nearly blind to everyone else.

That's definitely not me. Daiya *is* my friend, and I'd like to think I care for him, but I'm sorry to say that my feelings for him probably aren't strong enough to let me act so blindly. I could never be so focused on Daiya that I would dedicate a Box's wish entirely to him.

Daiya should understand as much if he ever stopped running away and faced the true owner.

But he couldn't.

Why?

Because the Box has made him lose sight of himself.

If he can't pinpoint the real owner, it's obvious he's in the wrong. If he doesn't even notice someone who thinks of him so intensely, Daiya is clearly at fault. He is consciously trying to forget this person in his attempt to turn his heart to stone. That's why he has shut himself off and blinded his own eyes.

And yet, he still claims to have some lofty purpose? To be offering his own life up without a second thought, trying to right the world?

"......Heh-heh."

It makes me laugh.

Ridiculous.

The efforts of such a person will never amount to anything.

Are you trying to suggest someone who's closed their eyes can indicate a proper course? They'll never point in the right direction. They'd only lead people even more astray.

And now he means to steal Maria from me?

Who the hell does he think he is?

"......"

I look at the unconscious Iroha, dyed in red. She was wrong, too. She tried to take Maria from me.

That's why I did this to her.

I told Haruaki she was alive, which is technically true, but I did rob her of her purpose in life. As her pitiful state now might suggest, she may never fully recover.

But who cares?

"......Heh-heh-heh."

Yep, I'm going to do the same thing to Daiya, too.

Daiya's despair will likely be even greater than Iroha's. This wish was originally his own. It'll be pretty much impossible to bounce back once he knows it'll never come true. What's more, Daiya murdered Koudai Kamiuchi. When he can't run anymore, the reality lying in wait for him is a cruel one.

But I'm going to crush him.

I don't give a rat's ass about the wish of some guy stumbling around in the dark. If the destruction of his Box leads him to a tragic fate, that's on him. That's just reaping what you've sown, right?

So.

Hurry up and give Maria back, you blind bastard.

15 Years Old and Earrings, SCENE 4, 1/3

1. A RIVERSIDE - DUSK

A bird's-eye view shot. The broad surface of the river sparkles in the light of the setting sun. It's a pure-red vista, except for the black silhouettes of two people. Their hands clasped together, the third-year middle schoolers Daiya and Kokone are facing forward, not looking at each other.

> KOKONE (VO)
> Daiya and I have always been together, for as long as I can remember.

Daiya squeezes the hand holding his firmly.

> KOKONE (VO)
> When I think back, he's always there in the images that appear in my head.

Their hands part.

> KOKONE (VO)
> If I want to put the past behind me, I have no choice but to break up with him.

2. *KOKONE'S ROOM - SIX MONTHS EARLIER, 5:00 PM*

The two of them sit on Kokone's bed in their
school uniforms.

> KOKONE
>
> Mm...f.

Daiya's lips move away from Kokone's. Her hair
is black, and she's wearing glasses. She looks down
shyly.

> KOKONE (VO)
> The two of us had always been together, but
> it was thanks to Haru that things changed
> between us. When Daiya saw Haru and me
> getting closer, he finally realized how he
> felt and initiated a relationship with me.
> From my standpoint, though, Daiya was too
> slow to realize how he felt.

Daiya intertwines his right hand with Kokone's,
then strokes her hair with the other. His gentle
smile sets Kokone's heart astir, and she presses her
head into his chest.

> KOKONE (VO)
> I had loved Daiya ever since we used to play
> house together, after all. I was well aware
> of my feelings, but I was just as aware that
> Daiya hadn't figured out his.

Daiya puts his arm around Kokone's back.

> KOKONE (VO)
> When I told Rino I'd had a crush on Daiya
> long before we started going out, she asked
> me if that really counted as being in love
> for a long time. She sounded so suspicious,
> but I think it did. At least, I was always
> infatuated with him in my memories. I lived
> my life constantly with it at the fore front

of my mind in the hopes that one day he would take notice of me.

An overview of Kokone's room appears. From the study desk to the CD player and stuffed animals, the room is full of pastel tones, with many white accents and furniture made of pale wood.

KOKONE (VO)
My room was full of Daiya. If I listened to a love song, it was his face that rose in my mind; if I read a romance manga, my feelings for him would overlap the protagonist's and bring me to tears. When I was studying, I would write *Kokone Oomine* in my notebook with a grin on my face. Daiya always filled my thoughts in my room.

DAIYA
Kokone.

KOKONE
What?

KOKONE (VO)
Daiya had recently started calling me by my first name. Obviously, I can remember the first time like it was yesterday. He was trying to play it cool, but he was blushing too hard to fool anyone. It's a memory I hold close to my heart even now.

DAIYA
I love you. I'll always love you, and that'll never change.

KOKONE
Yeah. I can believe that.

Daiya beams happily with an innocent, boyish smile. Kokone smiles in kind.

> KOKONE (VO)
> I have this feeling, deep in my heart. It's more than the empty promise of a girl silly in love; for me, it's a simple, certain truth.

Kokone runs her finger over Daiya's lips.

> KOKONE (VO)
> If it will make Daiya happy, I will give everything I am to him.

3. A RIVERSIDE - DUSK

Still wearing her sneakers, Kokone puts her feet into the river.

> KOKONE (VO)
> My world was warm. Warm like Daiya's body. Like one of those French movies I saw long ago. The world was so gentle, glowing pale and wrapped in sheer happiness.

Ever so slowly, Kokone slips into the dark-red water.

> KOKONE (VO)
> I was wrong, though. I had no idea. We all live on the same earth, but the truth is, I was the only one experiencing such kindness. I didn't know that it was completely different for everyone, that the world as others saw it might be cold or dirty or barbaric. And once I crossed paths with the worlds they saw—

Raw garbage floating down the river bumps up against Kokone's drenched form.

> KOKONE (VO)
> —my world would be corrupted, too.

Daiya enters the river, chasing after Kokone.

> KOKONE (VO)
> Hey, Daiya. Don't tie yourself down with promises that your love for me will never change. Your happiness brings me more joy than my own. I would do anything to make you happy. So you see—

Soaked in the river water, Daiya wraps his arms around Kokone.

> DAIYA
> Kokone, it'll be all right. I'll always be here with you.

Within Daiya's wet embrace, Kokone trembles.

> KOKONE
> You're cold.

Daiya releases her in a panic.

> KOKONE (VO)
> If I'm going to get in the way of your happiness, I'll make it easy for you to toss me aside.

◇◇◇ **Kazuki Hoshino 09/11 FRI 10:15 PM** ◇◇◇

I shouldn't let Daiya's Subjects find me.

What should my next move be? I'm still in the process of deciding what course to take, but it won't do for the Subjects to locate us. Haruaki and I put some distance between us and that tunnel under the elevated tracks. We can't stick around when Iroha's Subjects were just there.

We have no choice but to leave Iroha. Of course, it doesn't feel great to do, but we'd just create a scene carrying her back home all covered in fake blood; plus, it would cost us critical time. So as much as we hate to do it, we have to leave her until this is settled—just under two hours more.

We leave the tunnel and walk down the night streets. Until we decide on our next move, we'll go stay with Kokone.

"......Ya know, Hosshi, I wasn't sure whether to say this...," Haruaki begins, looking upset.

"Hmm? What's up?"

"You've just had this scary look in your eyes for a while now, you know? I know you're pissed at Daiyan. But you left Shindo back there, too. I'm okay with your reasons, but you didn't seem to care about her at all when you were explaining..."

"Huh?"

Maybe I did come across as cold?

I didn't even notice...but I wouldn't be surprised. It's hard to talk normally when your mind is busy screaming *Give Maria back, you blind bastard.*

"It's totally normal to be upset about losing Maria, but if you don't cool off, you're gonna screw up, ya know?"

"Yeah."

Calm down. Let's calm down and really think about how to get Maria back from Daiya.

"Another thing. I know this one is going to be tough to pull off, but...I really want to save Daiyan."

To be honest, that had slipped my mind. Everything had, except for Maria.

"...Yeah."

Of course, I want to help Daiya, too, if he's not beyond help already. But now, when I think of Maria, rage just boils up within me. I also can't help but feel that misplaced sympathies will make freeing Maria that much harder.

But not considering the option at all could very well lead to another failure. *Okay... Let's think of something else for now. Think of something that'll make me less angry with Daiya.*

"......Kokone."

Yeah.
My thoughts naturally turn toward Kokone Kirino.

It happened on September 9, two days ago.
Kokone asked me to come to her room.
I'd never been in her room before. At first glance, the black theme struck me as stylish and modern, but there was something weird about it, too. Nothing made it her own; its stylishness seemed like a facade, and Kokone herself didn't really fit the picture. It was as if she was following trends, as if she believed this was the kind of room she was supposed to have.
Knowing what I knew about Kokone, I couldn't help but think:
This room was meant to help her change.
To erase Daiya from her mind.
"...You don't need to hide it anymore. Tell me what Daiya did."
And yet, Kokone had given up on forgetting or ignoring Daiya. She had resolved to involve herself with him even more.
Seeing this, I thought:
What a relief.
I had intended to talk to her about Daiya even if she hadn't invited me here... No, I never had any other choice. If I was going to challenge Daiya, it would be impossible to ignore Kokone. And I wouldn't be able to keep it a secret from her anyway.
So I was grateful Kokone had prepared herself and let me know she was willing to hear me out.
After all, I would have kept the painful truth hidden from her if I could have, but I had no choice but to tell her.
—The past when Daiya was mistaken.
—The present when he was suffering.
—The future when he would be destroyed.
If she knew, Kokone would blame herself.
If she knew, she would be hurt.

If she knew, that pain would continue for some time to come.

I told her, though.

I told her everything about Daiya, no holding back.

Kokone couldn't speak another word for the rest of the day.

After I finished saying my piece, all she could do was stare at the wall behind me in a daze.

She didn't move, except for her chest rising and falling with each breath. I left the room, unable to do anything for her.

The next day, Kokone called me back again. Though her eyelids were a bit puffy when I came in and we said our hellos, nothing seemed out of the ordinary.

But the moment I closed the door, she undid the buttons of her shirt and started pulling it off.

It was all so sudden that I couldn't react. Maybe I should have looked away, but I couldn't even remember that I could. Dumbfounded, I just stood rooted to the spot in front of the door.

Kokone's face was blank as she turned her back toward me, now wearing only a bra on her upper body.

"Look."

At what? I was about to ask, but I spotted it before I could.

That "symbol" beneath the hook of her bra.

It was a burn mark, and not an accidental one. The scar looked like the kind you get by pressing a lit cigarette to your skin to prove how tough you are. And it wasn't just one. It was as if someone had illegally dumped a bunch of bulky garbage into a virgin snowy field. That's how many dozens of violent and painful burn marks there were.

These dozens of burns formed a symbol.

A symbol with connotations so obscene, you don't even see it in public restrooms these days.

"___"

It was enough to crush me. My emotions shattered under the pressure. That mark had me reeling.

"Hic... Ngh..."

The weight seemed to wring the tears out of me, almost against my will.

The image brought me to tears completely by reflex, so it wasn't until after I was already crying that I started thinking of how cruel it was, how painful, how she would most likely never be able to totally erase it, how this must have been the wedge that drove her and Daiya apart.

Kokone didn't really react to my sobbing; she just turned back around and chirped, "Think of the perks. You got to see me and my E cups in a bra."

As Kokone cracked a joke, as she normally would...she was crying.

Both of us were in tears throughout the rest of our conversation.

"My childhood friend Rino did this to me."

Kokone began telling me about the symbol as she buttoned up her shirt.

"Daiya's hot, obviously, and he had amazing grades, so all the girls loved him back then. He didn't have the silver hair or earrings, and he wasn't nearly as harsh, either. They even called him a prince. I wasn't a good match for him back then. My hair was black and dull and super-heavy, and my bangs were bluntly cut straight across. I had boring thick glasses, too. I was the classic plain girl. You'd probably find it hilarious if you saw a picture, huh? ...I can't really laugh, though."

I shook my head.

"Whether you were a good match has nothing to do with it. Daiya wouldn't care about that in the slightest."

"Yeah. It didn't matter to him." Having finished buttoning her shirt, Kokone looked at me. "But it did for the girls who were interested in Daiya."

I began to pick up on where that symbol had come from.

"...So Rino or whoever was upset that you weren't pretty enough for Daiya?"

"No, it didn't really bug Rino that much."

"So why?"

"Um, let's take it one step at a time. First, there's Rino. She was a year younger than me, and she was both my friend and Daiya's from child-hood. She'd had a crush on Daiya for a long time, too, just not as long as I had. She gave up on him, though, and started going out with a guy named Kamiuchi. The one Daiya…murdered, I guess."

I was stunned. I never knew that sort of connection existed between Daiya and Koudai Kamiuchi. Daiya hadn't seemed to pay him much mind even within the Game of Indolence.

But judging by the outcome, I couldn't help but think, *That's why Daiya chose to end things the way he did.*

"Kamiuchi did something horrible to Rino. I'm not really sure why he did it, but it hurt Rino a lot. So she started hitting on Daiya to try to heal, since she had liked him for so long.

"The thing is, by that time, Daiya and I were already in a relationship. Daiya liked me and not Rino. He was nice to her, but not any nicer than you'd normally be to an old friend. Rino picked up on this and got hurt even more. She just got worse and worse. She wasn't herself anymore, and she decided I had to pay for scheming to take Daiya all for myself."

Kokone had been crying the entire time, and she paused to blow her nose.

But her tears didn't stop.

"Rino said she went out with Kamiuchi because of me. She told me that what had happened to her was my fault. That's why she couldn't forgive me. She really believed all her suffering was my fault."

"And she did that to your back to punish you…?"

"Yeah. But if it were only Rino, I don't think she would've gone this far."

"Which means…"

"Yeah, it was more than one person. The problem wasn't Rino herself, but all the people around her who hated me, too. I think the biggest factor is that nobody pointed out that she was being crazy, which allowed things to escalate."

At last, the significance of what Kokone had said at the beginning dawned on me.

"You mean the people who were bothered because you and Daiya didn't 'match'?"

"Yeah. 'Bothered'…doesn't even begin to cover it. To them, it was the worst crime I could have committed. In their eyes, I was irredeemable for keeping their prince Daiya all to myself."

...What the hell?

The worst crime? I didn't get it.

Kokone and Daiya were going out because they liked each other—that's all.

"That... That's insane, any way you think of it. You didn't do anything wrong."

"Whether I was in the wrong didn't matter. What it comes down to is that some people out there will decide they don't like something, and they have to do something about it. It doesn't matter that the feeling just comes from their own jealousy; they certainly won't ever realize it. If you tell yourself a person you despise is the worst kind of monster, attacking them is easy."

"How could they think of you as a monster when you hadn't done anything bad?"

"It's simple. All they needed to do was cook up some reasons. Like, I didn't say hi to them, I always looked down on them, I always flirted with guys, I was flaunting my great relationship with Daiya, I seduced Daiya with my body, whatever. From there, they just bad-mouthed me in the group and kept agreeing with one another until the evil Kokone became an established fact in their minds. People can do it completely subconsciously. They built me up as a villain and then assaulted me to get it out of their system."

I suddenly recalled the two classmates of ours who had been talking about Kokone behind her back.

Those two had seemed to be talking trash about her out of envy. They didn't like Kokone for being popular with boys, so as that feeling had come to the forefront, they had started saying bad things about her to vent. It's possible they didn't like that Kokone was close with Daiya, either.

After what she had gone through, it's no wonder she couldn't let them get away with it.

"Rino had it in her to do this to me because she had been exposed to that atmosphere. They had no idea they were doing anything wrong. To them, baddies should have to suffer a little pain. Maybe they even thought it was just. They didn't think it was crazy, at least, and that's why they were able to do something so cruel."

"But that's... If they could look at themselves objectively, they would have to have realized they were nuts."

"They had turned their minds off, so they couldn't have."

"...Turned their minds off?"

"Yeah. Daiya said it a lot. That they had turned their minds off."

Yeah.

It's what Daiya loathes.

He believes that people who stop thinking are the ones who destroy what they have. It's why he's even using a Box to eliminate those kinds of people. He's trying to make a just world where things like what befell Kokone will never happen again.

"About a month or so after, I guess their minds started working again, because some people finally realized what they had done and apologized to me. But what was the point? It's not like I was going to forgive them, right? 'Sorry' wasn't going to make the scars go away. There was no meaning to it unless they'd realized what they were doing to me right then and there. It was so shameless, just apologizing so they could feel better about themselves... I told them so, and they came back with 'Isn't that a bit uncalled for? I'm here saying sorry?' Oh, rot in hell, bitch."

As she ranted and cursed, Kokone was, of course, still crying the entire time.

"Even if they apologized, there was no coming back for me. There was a time when I couldn't hate anyone, but that's gone forever."

And then, she said it:

"There was no coming back for my relationship with Daiya, either."

And yet—I didn't understand.

"Why?"

"Hmm?"

"Why did you need to break up with Daiya? Didn't he still love you even with that on your back? Didn't he try to help you heal? Why did you have to call it off with him?"

Kokone fell silent.

Sniffling a bit, she stared at the ceiling. She must have been doing her best to put her thoughts in order.

I realized it only once the words were out of my mouth, but my question may have been cruel. Was there really a reason to ask her that?

I mean, the two of them had already split up. Explaining why they ended it would definitely not be easy for her. I regretted saying anything.

Eventually, Kokone asked, "Kazu, am I...cute?"

"Huh?"

She was suddenly talking as she always did; maybe she was avoiding my question because she didn't want to answer it.

"Am I really all that pretty?"

But the look on her face was so earnest, it almost hurt.

I hadn't the faintest idea why she would be asking me with such desperation. Her expression let me know that I had to be careful with my response.

"...You are."

"Really?"

"Yeah. And you're not making me say that; it's my honest opinion. I'm not the only one who thinks so, either. It's obvious you're popular with the guys, isn't it? Didn't you say before that you've gotten so many love confessions, it's in the double digits?"

"That's true. I am a hottie, aren't I? I am cute. I'm in the same league as Daiya now."

"Out of his league, honestly."

"Ah-ha-ha, you're right. Daiya's got that delinquent aura now, so I'm the hotter commodity! After all, I'm a sweet high school girl, and an E cup to boot! No one can top that!"

But after that confident declaration, her forced grin faded, and her lips trembled.

".......But it's no good." She'd held back her tears for a moment, but they spilled over again.

"N-no good...?"

"I...can't get rid of this feeling that I'm ugly. This idea that I'm a worthless, subhuman animal won't go away."

"Wh-why? There's no reason for you to—"

"I know! I know I'm pretty enough! I'm well aware! I've done everything I can to make sure of it! I've worked so hard, believing that everything would be okay if I could just be pretty!"

Kokone grabbed my arm tight.

"But it didn't work...! That feeling won't go away, even though I know it's not true! I can't stop thinking I'm ugly! I can't shake the idea that I'm less than human, that I could never, ever be good enough for Daiya! Nothing helps! Not objective fact or subjective opinion!"

"S-so why is that?"

"Because that's what happens! I mean, they honestly believed I was some sort of inhuman monster. Do you think that wouldn't affect me? And I was a quiet, reserved girl back then, right? So that didn't help. After they looked at me like I was trash, after they burned me with lit cigarettes, after they berated me and said things like 'This is what you get for being a hag' or 'You're a witch who's no good for Daiya,' how could I say with confidence that I was worth anything as a person? I couldn't. It wasn't possible. So many people came and did horrible things to me. They honestly believed I was worthless, so of course they treated me like I was, you know? I even started thinking they might be right. Maybe it was normal for something that awful to happen to me. It had to be, or else none of it made any sense. This mark robbed me of all my self-confidence and dignity."

A belief that persisted even in the face of facts.

I think I had yet to understand that people could leave themselves so blind to the truth.

I did know one thing, though.

At that moment, Kokone was squeezing my arm so tight, it really hurt.

"I felt like if things didn't change, my self-hatred was going to kill me. And so, and so—"

Kokone wiped away her tears.

"—I had to beat it!"

There was no other option for her. If she didn't, she would break.

"I had to change! I had to throw away who I was in the past!"

That's why Kokone started wearing contact lenses, colored her hair, and adopted the latest styles. She put on a cheery personality and tried to become popular. She even succeeded. By sneering down at those who began to recognize her worth, who'd envied and bad-mouthed her, Kokone attempted to recover her self-confidence.

And yet, those things that had taken root in her heart would not disappear. She couldn't recover what the symbol had stolen.

So—

"I had to get rid of the me that cared so much for Daiya, too!"

If he was always going to be associated with what had come before, she would have to discard the part of her past that he embodied, too.

Kokone finally noticed she was squeezing my arm and let go of it.

"...Sorry, Kazu."

I shook my head.

I'm the one who should feel bad for making you talk about it.

Kokone took a deep breath to calm herself down.

"It's not like I wanted to break up with Daiya. It's just that, well, it wouldn't work. The truth is, a hug from him was already too much for me. The past would just come rushing back, all at once. Like a semitruck bearing down on me. I would get hot and start to hurt, just like when they jammed those cigarettes into my back, and it would remind me I had no worth as a human being. I can't get rid of that feeling. That's why being with Daiya...hurts."

Quite simply, they just couldn't stay together.

That was what ended things between them.

That's awful.

It was the only thought that came to mind.

As my head hung with sadness, Kokone suddenly said something to me.

"Hey, Kazu, you said you liked me once, right?"

"Um, huh?"

Why would she ask me that now? I thought, looking at her. I couldn't read the intentions behind her smile.

I...never said I liked her. That was something that person who had taken over my body did, not me.

But I hadn't yet explained that to her, so to Kokone, I *had* confessed my feelings to her.

"I was confused. I was happy that you said you liked me. You were the first one who made me feel that way. I thought maybe going out with you would be for the best. You would probably accept me even after you saw the burns on my back, too."

"...Look—" I started trying to tell her the truth, but Kokone cut me off.

"I thought if I went out with you, maybe Daiya would be able let me go, too."

I swallowed.

I didn't know the right thing to say, so I waited for Kokone's reaction.

"Anyway, I never would have suspected that Maria started it!"

...Now that she mentioned it, we still hadn't done anything to set the record straight, so the lie was still intact.

"S-sorry... Um, I can say this now, but that was actually the work of a Box. Maria fibbed to get the situation under control..."

"...Oh, I see. It was a Box's fault. That finally explains why things felt odd back then. Man, those Boxes really do cause a lot of trouble... But maybe, in the end, it was a good thing, you know? I think I needed to seriously consider having a relationship with you."

"That's... Um, why?"

"Look, Kazu. Do you remember how I cried in the music room?"

"Yeah."

That was when I came to, after Daiya had punched me. I heard later that the person trying to steal my body hadn't been satisfied with just telling Kokone I loved her; she had tried to rush the answer.

"I sincerely thought it would be best for the both of us if we started seeing other people. I honestly believed I would if I got the chance. And I got that opportunity when you came along and said you had feelings for me. I imagined myself with you, and Daiya with another girl. Then, when I looked at Daiya—"

She smiled bitterly.

"When I did, I couldn't stop myself from crying."

The smile didn't last long.

"That's how I knew."

Her face bunched up in genuine sadness and pain as she told me:

"I'm in love with Daiya."

I don't want to admit it. I don't want to admit how I feel, she must have thought, over and over again.

That was the meaning behind the pain on her face.

"The truth is...I wanted Daiya to only have eyes for me."

After all, once she admitted it, she wouldn't be able to wish for Daiya's happiness.

"Even if you and I started dating, my feelings for Daiya wouldn't go away, I knew. And I could also tell that it would be the same for him. No matter what we tried, our problems would never be solved unless I became the girl I used to be. Nothing will be fixed unless I can accept him like I once did. I can't see myself ever being able to, but it's the only thing that would work."

It's a tragedy.

"It was more than Daiya could take."

The world had changed, but they hadn't.

They couldn't accept reality.

"That's why he turned to the Box. And no matter how you look at it—"

Unable to take it any longer, Kokone pressed her forehead against my shoulder.

"No matter how you look at it, everything that's happened with Daiya is my fault!"

I couldn't see her expression.

"That's why I'll do anything. If it'll save Daiya, I will do anything. If a Box is what it takes to save him, then I'll get one. I'd give my life as many times as it takes to help him."

Something she said troubled me, and I repeated it without thinking.

"...Give your life?"

"Yes, I'm not lying."

She was probably right.

It wasn't a lie.

Kokone would give her life to save Daiya.

She already had.

If she had gotten ahold of a Box instead of Daiya, then a different, yet similar, disaster would have occurred.

Their feelings for each other are destroying both of them.

Their love is at once beautiful and horrific.

What if?

What if the incident that created that burn on Kokone's back never happened?

If that were the case, there would have been no problem whatsoever in their love. It would have stayed an enviable, beautiful romance. No ugliness or anything of the sort. The two of them would have cared for each other and spent their days together in happiness.

Just a single unfortunate event ruined that framework.

If only one of those tiny details had been different. What if Rino weren't their childhood friend? If Rino and Koudai Kamiuchi hadn't gotten together? If Koudai Kamiuchi didn't do those horrible things to Rino? If Kokone and Daiya had kept their relationship a secret? If Kokone's personality were a little more forceful? If someone had been there to stop her mistreatment? If Daiya had noticed Rino's alarming behavior? If Haruaki had displayed his affections for Kokone more openly? If I had been friends with all of them in middle school? All it would have taken was a tiny difference to change their fate so completely that they would have been smiling right about now.

Even I could imagine that. I wondered how many hundreds of times Kokone and Daiya had gone through those "what-ifs" in their heads.

They must have despised this world. It singled them out to experience so much malice and destroyed what they had, all without allowing them the opportunity for a single trifling "what-if."

And that's why Daiya began this reckless struggle to purify our heartless world.

…But what about Kokone?

"Kokone."

"Yeah?"

She still had her forehead pressed against my shoulder.

"If you did get a Box, how would you use it?"

"I'd use it for Daiya. I'd wish for a world where he can smile and be happy."

But that future no longer existed.

Daiya had already passed the point of no return.

That wish would never be fulfilled, and I was sure Kokone knew it.

"I wonder if it'd work, though? Could it come true without any weird, random thoughts being included, too?"

That's why she said what she said.

Lifting her head up at last, Kokone smiled feebly and said something that made me certain she would never return to who she was before.

"Could I wish for it without thinking that everyone besides Daiya should die?"

"Oh, that's not what I meant! Sorry, sorry! I would never want you to die, Kazu! Oh, and Haru, too, of course! I really like Haru, you know?"

Kokone had quickly corrected herself, but I couldn't be sure she actually meant it. So I had to ask her something. She had said she really liked Haruaki, so I needed to hear her answer.

"Have you ever thought of going out with Haruaki?"

Kokone's eyes had gone round.

Then she had smiled sadly.

Oh, I see; she really did know how Haruaki felt.

"I have," Kokone had said casually, acting as if it were nothing at all. *"It wouldn't work out, though. Haru knows about my past, too."*

"What're you giving me that weird look for, Hosshi?"

Haruaki watches me with a frown as we walk through the night.

I remember what he had confessed to me once before:

"I used to have a crush on Kiri.

"But you know what? She's changed. I don't feel that way toward her at all now, see?

"I think you should go out with her. You guys are a good fit."

Haruaki must've known.

He can't help Kokone. He knows about her past, so he would be someone who brought her suffering, just like Daiya.

Maybe that's why, just like Kokone and Daiya, he told me I should go out with Kokone.

Even if I asked him, Haruaki would probably just brush it off with some excuse, though.

He may not even know the answer himself.

"...Hey, Haruaki." I ask him something else instead. "You said before that Kokone has lost heart, right?"

Haruaki is startled and stares at me.

But he lets out a single big breath, and his lips quickly turn up in a smile.

"Yeah, I did."

"What made you think that?"

Haruaki puts his hand to his chin for a moment in thought, then says, "Imagine this, Hosshi. A person is drowning right in front of you, and you can save them, no problem. If so, would you help them? I want you to really picture it, then answer."

I conjure up the image. Someone is drowning out at sea or somewhere. I imagine a little boy crying out in desperation, his arms flailing. I pick up a life jacket or the like, and I can save him without putting myself in any real danger.

"Sure I'm gonna help them."

"Why?"

"What do you mean, why? Obviously, I want to help them if I can, right? There's no specific reason. And...yeah. I think I would regret it if they died right in front of me when I could've helped them. I'd probably be traumatized. I'd never forget it for the rest of my life."

"Right? Same here."

It's the obvious conclusion.

But if he's asking me this question now—

"Are you implying it's different for Kokone?"

"No, she said she would help them."

"What?"

I'm surprised. The way the conversation has been going, I was positive it would be different for her.

However, Haruaki still has more to say.

"But when I asked Kiri that question, she asked me a question before she said she would help." Haruaki smiles weakly. "*What kind of person are they?*"

I don't get what's wrong with that question right away.

But then it starts to dawn on me.

"If someone is drowning in front of you, and it's in your power to save them, you'd want to do it unconditionally. It's someone drowning, after all, so you should imagine someone powerless, who needs rescuing."

It's conceivable that some people out there might ask the same question as Kokone for no real reason.

Haruaki would probably not be telling me this if Kokone's response hadn't meant something, though. If he's going to the trouble of mentioning it, to him, it's a sign of something abnormal.

"But Kiri, she doesn't see someone simply in need of help. The first thing she does is suspect that their drowning might be a ploy to hurt her. Kiri can't even relax enough to help someone on the verge of drowning unless she can confirm they aren't hostile toward her first. She lives her life experiencing a level of suspicion neither of us could believe. That's what would keep her from acting. Even though if that person did drown, she would be just as sorry about it as we would, for the rest of her life."

What prompted Haruaki to ask Kokone in the first place?

Was it because he suspected she would answer that way already, to an extent? Because he already understood this side of her and asked her only to confirm it?

"Since she's been bullied, Kiri considers strangers hostile. She has her guard up right from the get-go. That's what prevents her from doing what she should. She hates what happened to her, hates everything about herself that allowed it to happen. Her negativity has her captive. She's so tied up in it, she can't do what she wants or needs to do. To me, it—"

Haruaki pauses briefly, out of breath, then finishes:

"It means she's lost hope."

I can tell from what he's saying.

Haruaki still cares for Kokone.

You see, he has a better grasp of the darkness within her than I do after hearing about it from her directly. He wouldn't know about it unless he's kept her in his thoughts this entire time.

In a somewhat defeated tone, Haruaki says, "Kiri will never change as long as she can't put her own happiness first."

I know what Haruaki wants: not to go out with Kokone himself, but for her and Daiya's relationship to be restored. He wants her to be with the boy she loves, to spend her life with him, to be with someone who sees things her way, to find happiness together.

A thought enters my head.

—*Put your own happiness first.*

That's what Haruaki says she has to do.

But he hasn't managed to do that, either.

A correct solution.

If I could begin to sketch a solution for the three of them, what would the outline be?

All three going back to how they once were. No one could complain about that outcome.

But it's not possible. It's not possible even with a Box capable of granting any wish.

All we can do is find a new, ideal relationship for the three of them...or at least one that's acceptable.

I have yet to puzzle out how to do that, though.

I'm sure the trio in question doesn't know, either.

I can't see the shape of our goal. Which means I can't take action toward those ends.

What I do know is that as long as Daiya's Crime, Punishment, and the Shadow of Crime is still around, that solution will never take shape.

Oh, but that's nothing more than an excuse. I'm not trying to deceive myself.

I act for Maria's sake. I can't do it for my three friends Daiya, Kokone, and Haruaki. I'm destroying Crime, Punishment, and the Shadow of Crime not for their salvation, but to rescue Maria and complete my mission.

Helping them is not something I can do. I can only hope for a happy future for Daiya and the others after I accomplish what I've set out to do.

That hope is sincere, though.

I can't see the solution now, but I still make this prayer with the faith that we'll find it.

"Are you okay with that, Haruaki?" I whisper.

".........Hmm?"

I didn't mean to be heard, but it seems Haruaki did in fact hear it.

"It's nothing."

I've sorted myself out. I'm calm. I'll put all my strength into what I can do now.

I will stomp out Daiya's twisted wish.

Yes, I exist to crush others' wishes.

"Haruaki, what do you think our next step should be?" I ask, now that I've figured out what I need to do.

"Wellll... If we're playing it safe, then I guess maybe just wait for the Silver Screen of Broken Wishes to finish doing its thing."

"That probably is the way to go, huh?"

But I'm not so positive, and I can tell Daiya's thinking the same thing. We know the score. We also know Daiya has probably guessed Haruaki and I would choose to wait things out, so he'll more than likely use his smarts and his Box to take down the Silver Screen of Broken Wishes.

We're running up on the time limit. As that happens, Daiya will probably become less and less picky with his tactics. He'll try to use Crime, Punishment, and the Shadow of Crime to drive me against a wall. Just like when he searched for Maria and me, he will employ his nearly one thousand Subjects.

Having a thousand people tracking me down had been pretty terrifying, like being under surveillance by the entire world.

The next Order will be more than a search to spook me. Worst case, it's not crazy to think Daiya might issue an Order to kill the person he thinks is the owner. He might go so far as to have me killed, too. Nearly one thousand people are going to come after me in a direct attack.

Of course I'm shaking.

They say a cornered mouse will bite a cat, but Daiya is no mouse. It's a lion we've got cornered here. If I screw up even slightly, he'll spring back from the brink and crush me in his jaws in one fell swoop.

"What should we do...?"

"Your only choice is to hide, don't you think? Can't really launch an attack if you can't find the target," Haruaki suggests. He's right. "Even with a thousand or so people on the lookout, they probably can't sniff out someone in hiding in just two hours, right? Using the Internet like they did last time wouldn't be very effective in such a short amount of time, either... Plus, if you're going to lie low, then Kiri should, too. There's no telling when Daiyan will start considering the possibility that Kiri is the owner... Whoa, I was just throwing out ideas, but that might be a good one, even for me. If you're hiding out with Kiri now, we may just get through this yet."

As it happens, Kokone is hiding in a dormitory; it belongs to the baseball team of a friend of another friend Haruaki met through his own ball team. Haruaki was there, too, until just a while ago.

We moved Kokone there after Yuri filled us in on the details of Crime, Punishment, and the Shadow of Crime. Our thinking was that the Subjects would be less likely to track her down if she was tucked away in the home of some loosely connected acquaintance rather than out in the open. Daiya doesn't even know said acquaintance exists, let alone where the dorms are.

I'm positive we could stay hidden for a little under two hours.

But if we do—

"Daiya isn't going to let us stay in hiding."

Yep, there's no way in hell that Daiya will allow it under these circumstances.

"He'll come up with some way to lure us out. If he threatens Maria as bait to call me out again, I won't have any choice but to play along."

"Ugh! I see..."

"......Hmm? But..." And I get an idea. "...Yeah. So if that's how it's going to be, then how about we just don't let him make any threats...?"

Haruaki tilts his head at my raised voice.

"Huh? What do you mean by that? Isn't it up to him whether he makes a threat?"

"Here's what we need to do." I pull out my cell phone and turn it off.

"...? How is that going to stop him from threatening you?"

"Can't threaten me if you can't get in touch. He can order me to come meet him, but there's no point if he can't get ahold of me."

"Okay? I get that, but if Daiyan is trying to hurt Maria, whether he gets in contact with you doesn't change the fact that she's in danger, does it? You just wouldn't know about it. Heck, you'd be ignoring it."

"Daiya doesn't have any reason to want to harm Maria, does he? If he says he's going to, it's really just a reason to call me out. If he can't even do that, though, there's no point in hurting Maria."

"...I hear you."

"So the first thing I'm gonna do is hide, as you suggested. Then I'm gonna make it so I can't get any messages from Daiya. Once I've done that—"

"Daiyan can't work any plots to draw you out! Which means you can wait it out! ...If that's what we're doing, then Kiri and I will need to turn our phones off, too. He may not be able to reach you on your phone, but if he can reach us, that means he can reach you. All right, I'm going to tell Kiri to turn her phone off, and then I will, too."

Haruaki begins entering a text.

A thought enters my mind. Would I have been better off if I had come up with this idea sooner?

Would I have had an easier time if I had?

...But maybe not.

If I were the only one involved, cutting off all contact would have been a viable strategy. But I had to protect Maria. If she were placed in danger, letting things pass in ignorance would not have allowed me to avoid the crisis itself.

In a certain sense, this is a move I can make only now that I don't have Maria holding me back. A move I can make because, like Daiya, I have my back against the wall.

"Okay. Let's hurry and meet up with Kokone and go off the radar before the Subjects find us."

"Hell yeah. Now that we've got that settled, let's go ahead and—"

Haruaki's cheery reply stops short.

"Haruaki?"

He is standing stock-still, eyes glued to the screen of his phone.

"......Don't tell me Daiya already reached out to you?"

Not replying, Haruaki starts clicking at his phone with a stern expression. He starts up the app for 1seg TV broadcasts and watches the screen intently.

...Why TV at a time like this?

But Haruaki begins searching for something as if unable to find the video he wants.

"Haruaki, what's the matter?"

"...There's something on the TV Kiri told me in her text to watch. It looks like it's already ended, though. She's panicked, too."

Going quiet again, Haruaki looks me in the face, perhaps having at last come across the video he was looking for.

"......Hosshi, I think we're too late."

He shoves his phone out at me.

On the screen is a news program that has been uploaded to a video site. It's the weather forecast, broadcast live from a street downtown.

"—Urk."

But there's something wrong in this weather report.

A naked woman. A thin woman with brown hair, probably in her fifties, has gotten on all fours and started barking. She is crouched, so it's hard to see, but beneath her hanging breasts, large words have been written in permanent marker.

Come to the movie theater.

She appears for only a moment before the screen jerks and switches back to the studio. That's where the video ends.

"...Hosshi, can we really ignore Daiyan if he's even using TV to make his threats? ...There's no way."

"You're right... It won't work."

What if, for example, Daiya made one of his Subjects say *I'll kill Maria Otonashi if you don't come to the theater*? It wouldn't make any difference to Daiya whether his message actually reached us or not. Now that he's gone this far, he might really follow through on his threat with the *expectation* that we have received his message.

As long as there's a risk of that, we can't ignore him.

If we still persist with this plan, he'll only go to even more extreme lengths to reach us. He may even utilize his Subjects to ensure I could never have a normal life ever again.

In the worst-case scenario, the Daiya we're dealing with now could harm Maria.

Now that he's discovered this method, I can't avert my eyes from him any longer. Even indirect threats will work on me now.

"Urgh!"

As it stands, *not* noticing messages from Daiya will be the problem. I don't see the point in keeping this up now. I turn my phone back on.

Instantly, I receive a call, as if it were just waiting for me.

Opening my phone, I check the name on the screen.

Kasumi Mogi.

"Found youuu."

I haven't answered the phone. After all, it's still ringing from the incoming call.

I can hear another sound besides my stupid electronic ringtone, one I'm not used to hearing.

Roll, roll, roll.

It's the sound of wheels.

The sound of a wheelchair.

◆◆◆ Daiya Oomine 09/11 FRI 10:12 PM ◆◆◆

I never limit myself to just one scheme.

I had trusted in Iroha Shindo's capability, but that's not to say I've been operating under the assumption that she would guarantee success. If I did happen to rely on the actions of someone else and something unexpected happened, it could prove fatal, given the unforgiving time constraints.

That's why my plan didn't rely solely on Shindo when I was putting the screws to Kazu during the third movie, *Repeat, Reset, Reset.* I had several other ploys in the works while she was "revealing Kazu's betrayal to Otonashi."

One of them consisted of messages to Kazu on TV using dog-people. I issued an Order to eleven of my Subjects who had committed grave enough crimes that I wouldn't mind making dog-people of them. The

Order was to write *Come to the movie theater* on their naked bodies and show it to Kazuki by displaying their disgraceful state on television. While I haven't yet confirmed if it was actually carried out or not, I'm sure one or two of them succeeded.

Aya's arrival here made me think that attempt was a wasted effort, but by the same token, her presence gives it new importance.

Thanks to this, I can prevent Kazu and the others from cutting off contact with me.

From Kazu's perspective, all he needs to do to bring me down is wait for the Silver Screen of Broken Wishes to reach its conclusion, meaning there's a good chance he'll cut off all contact with me and go into hiding. But a broadcast mishap of that magnitude would make waves across the Internet and elsewhere, making it extremely likely to reach Kazu's ears. And once it did, Kazu would understand the dangers of cutting off contact.

If I can reach him, then I can use Crime, Punishment, and the Shadow of Crime more effectively in this conflict.

We're in the entrance. *15 Years Old and Earrings* has yet to start. I'll lose pretty much all freedom once the show begins, so I have to use this time to put together the broad brushstrokes of a plan.

There are seventeen minutes left until the movie starts. We'll be teleported to the theater five minutes before, so that leaves twelve minutes. Dammit... Not much time, but what else is new?

"In other words, this is what you're saying your plan is."

Aya summarizes what I just finished telling her.

"Kasumi Mogi is experiencing despair because of her physical condition and her unrequited romantic feelings for Kazuki Hoshino. If I ask her if she wants to use the Misbegotten Happiness, she won't say no. So I'll use my Box on Mogi, thus forgetting about Kazuki Hoshino."

I nod, and Aya continues.

"Kazuki Hoshino probably hasn't explained the Boxes to Mogi and had her join his side. I doubt he'd want to tell Mogi about them, since she took such pains to wipe the Rejecting Classroom from her mind. Plus, a paraplegic just wouldn't be much help to him in this fight. Basically, if you can bring a Subject in contact with her, your plan can move forward without any harm coming to her. And getting in touch will be easy. She has to be at the hospital, after all."

Well, to be honest, I couldn't care less about Mogi. I just want Kazu to come to the Silver Screen of Broken Wishes, but there's no need for me to say that.

"Kasumi, huh...?"

That useless, annoying idiot butts in yet again. *Shut the hell up, you teru teru bozu bitch.*

"...You're thinking something rude, aren't you? It's all over your face. I'm good at reading expressions, you know?"

Against my will, I converse with Yanagi for a bit. "...Just asking, but do you know Mogi?"

"Well, she's both my rival in love and an ally against a shared enemy. I sometimes trade info with her at the hospital. Eh-heh-heh."

"So, discussing the perfect crime for how to bump off Otonashi? Is your switcheroo trick using the wheelchair almost complete? Everyone knows Mogi can't get around on her own, so who'd have thought you'd take advantage of that to craft your alibi."

"Why is your murder plan so specific?! You really need to rethink your image of me!"

"And while we're at it, why did you butt in when Mogi came up? You got something on your mind?"

"Huh? ...Um, no..."

Ugh, I shouldn't have asked. Time to put this girl out of my mind.

"Now, then." *How to go about using Mogi...*

Nevertheless, Aya is better bait for Kazu than Mogi. It's a simple plan, but using a Subject in the outside world to threaten Kazu about Aya is the best option. The threat will go something like this:

If you don't smash the Silver Screen of Broken Wishes by the end of today, I'll kill Maria Otonashi.

I should probably set the time limit to five minutes or so before the end of the day at midnight. Threats are effective. Desperate as I am, there is no way for Kazu to say for certain that I won't murder Aya.

If so, then what do I intend by using Mogi? Why do I find it necessary, even though putting her in the middle will take a not-so-negligible amount of extra time?

I do need to make Aya think of using the Misbegotten Happiness on poor, heartbroken Mogi. That's not the entirety of it, though.

As I thought just a moment ago, threats using Aya work.

The problem is, they work *too well*. It might suggest to someone that I'm going to win this.

To whom, you ask?

To O.

"As for how to get Kazu to come here, I've got an idea." I decide to try telling Aya about it.

"Let's hear it, then."

"I'll just have a Subject break Mogi's fingers."

"......What're you saying?" Aya scowls. Just as I thought.

"It's a threat: If you don't want to stay quiet and watch Mogi lose her hands, then come into the Silver Screen of Broken Wishes. Kazu once had feelings for her. Even he can take the sound of her fingers snapping for only so long, right? To make matters worse, Mogi can use only her upper body. Her hands are more important to her than to other people, right?"

"I won't let you do that, either!"

"Don't you hate Mogi? Didn't she stab you?"

"Don't make me repeat myself. My feelings have nothing to do with it. I can't stand by while people get hurt, no matter who they are."

Yep, that's pretty much the reaction I anticipated. There's not really any point in getting Aya worked up here.

"...Understood. Let's scratch that plan, then," I acquiesce. But I don't mean it.

It's not as if Aya ever had any means of checking what Orders I make, so I can get away with just saying this. No need for me to stay true to my word. Whether I have her blessing or not, what matters is that Mogi's fingers break.

This little script is not for Aya, but for O. I need to convince her that this is the trump card of my strategy.

If it's for Maria's sake, Kazu may very well leave Mogi to her broken-fingered fate. Kazuki Hoshino can veer that far off the path of common sense, once he's prepared for the worst.

I'm sure O thinks so, too. That's why she won't think I'll win with this gambit. If it appears that my stratagem is going to fail, then I doubt she'll step in.

In actuality, the center of my plan is a threat against Aya. I'll keep that fact under wraps, though, by convincing O that my threat revolves around Kasumi Mogi.

The question is whether I can pull it off when my opponent is O.

And I conclude:

—I can.

O can apparently observe the world. But as far as I can tell, this process is like using a satellite camera to peer down at the earth. It makes it difficult to get a detailed understanding of the motives behind my actions. That is O's weakness.

So I can do it. Like a magician distracting his audience with showmanship while he smoothly performs his sleight of hand, I can conceal my threat with Aya by making another one with Mogi.

Naturally, I can't rest easy and assume what someone as unpredictable as O will do. I'll need to adapt on the fly depending on how things play out.

The thing is, I'm beginning to get a grasp on how O's mind works. Though her almost godlike abilities made it difficult to see, now that I recognize her true nature—for better or worse—I can make the correct analysis.

O's personality is not something otherworldly like that of a god or demon, but something more mundane like that of an eccentric human being. Her mental acumen is apparently quite high, but nothing that breaches the bounds of common sense. Nothing special. I'm fairly certain her personality was based on a certain girl's image of her big sister, the real "Aya Otonashi."

So my analytical skill allows me to read her behavior for the most part.

For example, there's one thing of which I'm certain—sometime today, O will show up.

★   ★   ★

"………Iroha!"

I turn in the direction of Yanagi's sudden cry.

Standing beneath the electric billboard is Iroha Shindo, her school uniform red and dirty, her face exhausted and smeared with mud.

"Wh-what's wrong, Iroha? On your uniform—is that blood? Are you hurt?" Yanagi runs up to Shindo in concern.

"It's fake blood. I'm not injured, but…I might as well be dead."

"Wh-what do you mean?"

"My Box was broken." Yanagi's eyes go wide with surprise, while Aya's brows narrow intensely.

I have a heap of things I want to ask her, too. But there's something I have to say before I do so.

"Is this pathetic farce supposed to accomplish something, O?"

Yanagi and Aya look from O to me, their eyes still wide.

"……Oh?"

Shindo's expression goes from utter exhaustion to that familiar bewitching gentleness.

All the same—seeing that look brings something to mind, though it has no bearing on anything now.

That benevolence really does remind me of the expression Kazu had when he sent me into the Silver Screen of Broken Wishes.

"I must say, I'm hurt that you didn't let yourself be fooled for even a second. How on earth did you know it was me?"

"…It was just a hunch."

The truth is, I had predicted that O would make an appearance here before too long. Given her nature, O would probably want to see Kazu and me squirm.

I'm not going to say that answer aloud, of course. It's no good if O thinks I'll win. Being honest here would probably only set O on guard, and I don't need that.

O doesn't seem to have any particular doubts. Not even that interested, in fact.

"……O." Aya has been watching our interaction with what almost amounts to a glare. Her eyes are full of hatred.

"I haven't seen you in some time."

"I don't suppose you're planning to give me a new Box?"

"Surely there's no reason for me to do that? I'm certain I kindly informed you that as a subject for observation, you're hardly any different from a vacuum cleaner. I have no intention of meddling with something little different from a machine."

As I watch their exchange, I think:

What the hell is this charade?

Why does O claim to have no interest in Aya yet speak with such hostility? O doesn't respond to others like this. Why doesn't Aya find that suspicious?

Why can't Aya catch on to O's true nature?

My train of thought is cut off as O looks at me.

"Oomine. Actually, I need to speak with you. Is that acceptable?"

This proposal is unexpected. Unexpected because I had taken it for granted that O would remain an observer as long as Kazu didn't encounter any major setbacks.

I still have a ways to go when it comes to reading O. I glance at my watch as I pull myself together.

10:19 PM.

"I hope it's productive? I have less than six minutes of freedom to chat. If it's small talk you want, sorry."

If I do speak with O, it'll most likely take until I'm transported to the theater. Once that happens, I won't be free to act.

"It's something of importance to you."

That settles it. That alone prevents me from refusing O's offer out of hand.

"Understood."

All I would be able to do with Aya in my remaining time is go over my plans again anyway. I've already made the Order for Mogi. I've sent a Subject—a fanatical follower, in fact—to her hospital.

"Forgive me, but would the rest of you mind leaving the room? I must speak with Oomine alone."

Aya isn't happy about this. "Wait. Why do you and Oomine—?"

"Sorry." I rein Aya in. "But there's no time to have your question answered. Just hold on to it for now."

Though she's clearly upset about it, Aya doesn't say anything further.

★   ★   ★

The instant I can tell that Yanagi and Aya are gone, I start talking.

"Get to the point," I tell O-in-Shindo's-form. I genuinely don't have time for pleasantries.

"Hmph, very well," O agrees, then gives me the gist. "Kazuki and I are now enemies."

All my assumptions are shattered.

"_____"

I'm stunned. To be honest, I want time to spend going over the implications of what I've just heard. Unfortunately, I don't get a grace period.

The shock has left my emotions churning, but the question I ask is a productive one.

"So are you on my side?"

I can't put thoughts and feelings in order, but I can still at least make the proper B response to A. I don't have the time or resources to confirm the truth of O's claim or ask for the particulars. I just have to assume that statement is true and find out if this situation is useful to me.

"I will not be your ally."

"Why not? Kazu is our common enemy now, right?"

"I don't believe Kazuki will abandon hope if I go along with your way of doing things. To put it another way, I don't see any advantage in becoming your ally."

"Still, if you're against Kazu, that means you aren't going to interfere in my victory so he can win, correct?"

"That is true. I will not interfere. In fact, I have something nice to share with you. Your plan, the plan of using the Misbegotten Happiness in front of Kazuki to remove Maria Otonashi's memories of him, is the best option available to you at the moment. I guarantee that."

I don't have the time to confirm whether this is true, either. I just have to take it at face value.

"Next question. Kazu is supposedly more interesting to you than anyone else. Why is he your enemy now?"

"You speak as if my fascination means he can't become my foe, but it's quite the opposite. His position as my enemy is precisely what fascinates me about him."

"Enough with the flowery speech. What I'm asking is the *reason* he became your enemy."

"So brusque. If I exist to allow Maria Otonashi to be 'Aya Otonashi,' then Kazuki exists to erase 'Aya Otonashi' from Maria Otonashi. It's only natural that we oppose each other, don't you think?"

"I guess… Still, how does Kazu thinking that change anything? Just saying, Kazu may have some quirks, but he's only human. Are you saying a mere mortal like Kazu has the ability to do away with you, specifically?"

"Yes, he does. Kazuki has obtained the ability to crush Boxes by force."

That sure cuts off my ranting, as you might imagine.

"…The ability to crush Boxes?" What kind of cheating BS is that?

I think for a moment that O is referring to the Silver Screen of Broken Wishes, but no. That Box can crush only my Crime, Punishment, and the Shadow of Crime.

"Why does Kazu have this power?"

"Because he is another person who has gained power from the Misbegotten Happiness. Much like myself."

"I don't understand. How would Kazu gain power from the Misbegotten Happiness—? No, I'll just take that as it is. There's one thing I just can't reconcile, though, and that's *when* Aya got the Misbegotten Happiness. I don't know all the details, but Aya and Kazu weren't acquainted at that point, were they? If so, then how would it have influenced Kazu?"

"It's not really all that difficult. The Misbegotten Happiness was always going to make a force to counterbalance me. But as Maria Otonashi could not conceive of a being capable of opposing me, that position remained vacant. That doesn't mean there was no counterbalance at all, however. The post remained, ready to be filled. And then the one meant to take it appeared. The anomaly, Kazuki Hoshino, whom a certain someone saw as a savior. The discrepancy in the timing doesn't amount to all that much."

I see. In a sense, that discrepancy is even more characteristic of a Box.

As it happens, something has been bugging me for a little while now.

"I want to make sure of something."

"And what would that be?"

"What the hell are you?"

"What am I? Such a crude question. I'm afraid I can't humor you because the scope of the question is beyond my capacity to answer."

"I get that you're made in the image of the real Aya Otonashi, and that you've been influenced by the Misbegotten Happiness. What I can't figure out, though, is why Kazu is the force that opposes you, and why he has the power to remove you."

"Yes, I can see you don't understand yet. The Misbegotten Happiness is originally a Box that gives me existence as O. That's how it grants wishes. If it's destroyed, I can't exist as O."

I'm almost reeling from the shock, but there's no time for whirling emotions. I respond with pure logic.

"So what you're implying is that when I received a Box, I used Aya's Misbegotten Happiness, too?"

"Indeed. Without the Misbegotten Happiness, there would be no me."

"But wouldn't that mean Aya doesn't actually lose her memories when she uses the Misbegotten Happiness? I'm actually using the Box, but she hasn't forgotten anything."

"It's not a lie. The memory loss occurs only when she decides to use the Misbegotten Happiness of her own will."

"That's quite a convenient system."

"Is it? Haven't Boxes always worked this way? Give it some thought; can't you work out why she loses her memory to begin with?"

The question reminds me of the almost laughable conversation between O and Aya just a moment ago.

Why is Aya almost stupidly unaware of O's identity? I think.

The answer comes to me.

She has to be, or the Misbegotten Happiness could never come into existence.

Aya must never realize that O is the product of her own Box. Furthermore, she must never realize that O is like the real "Aya Otonashi." She must never know how her Box grants the wishes of other people. If she ever found out, the Misbegotten Happiness wouldn't just be "misbegotten," it would be a downright screwup.

So if she's going to learn how the Box works when she uses it, she has to forget.

O and Aya have been set to despise each other so that the Box won't create a broken wish. Aya has cooked up a story in which she is trying to get a new Box from her archnemesis so that this time, she can make a perfect wish that is not "misbegotten."

But it's not possible for Aya to obtain her ideal Box. It'll never be possible.

After all, her struggle against O *is* her entanglement in the Misbegotten Happiness.

"＿＿＿"

What the hell?

What sort of fool's errand is that? She may as well be building a sandcastle that will collapse under a little rain. Is this really what Aya has been persevering for? Is this what she has spent a whole lifetime on? Is this what she's killed off her own personality for, what she's staked her life on?

"……"

Does Kazu realize that Aya's battle is in vain? I'm sorry, but the way his head works, he probably doesn't know what exactly is going on.

I'm sure he gets the essence of it, though.

He has an intuitive grasp on the truth of this Box.

Yeah, that's how Kazuki Hoshino is.

That's why I know he'll try to crush the Misbegotten Happiness. He will attempt to deliver Maria Otonashi from this system of meaningless sacrifice.

And, it goes without saying, my Crime, Punishment, and the Shadow of Crime is standing in his way.

"What exactly does Kazu need to do to destroy Boxes? How would my Box be broken?"

"If Kazuki is able to touch your chest, he can remove your Box and crush it. That's how he did away with Iroha Shindo's Box, in fact."

"…What? He actually took out Shindo? …Wait, more importantly—"

All he has to do is touch me?

That's bad.

I just tried to send an invitation for Kazu to enter the Silver Screen of Broken Wishes.

But if he can crush Crime, Punishment, and the Shadow of Crime by just touching me after I've called him in here—

"I'm SOL, aren't I?"

If I do nothing here, the Silver Screen of Broken Wishes will destroy my Box. On the other hand, Crime, Punishment, and the Shadow of Crime will also be crushed if I summon Kazu here and let him get his hands on me. Give me a break. You can be only so unfair.

Let's think in specifics. When Kazu shows up in the Silver Screen of Broken Wishes, for instance, I could take Aya hostage and tie her head over my chest to prevent him from touching me.

That's not an option, though. It's not an issue of ethics—I just won't be able to do it. I'd be in the theater when it happens, and the Silver Screen of Broken Wishes makes me incredibly *lethargic* if I attempt to do anything other than watch the movie. I won't have the strength to resist that and hold down her head, not for long.

Does that mean our gambit to remove Aya's memories of Kazu with the Misbegotten Happiness is my only option, regardless of whether he comes here or not?

That won't work, either, though. Things won't go that smoothly. Aya has said she has no intention of using the Misbegotten Happiness on anyone who doesn't want it, and she's not likely to bend on that. I don't have time to hatch some plot to make Yanagi or Mogi desperate enough to ask her to use it. And my Box will be crushed if Kazu touches me in the meantime.

...But if the power of the Misbegotten Happiness has always been the power to grant the use of O's Boxes, then there is something that makes me wonder.

"Can the Misbegotten Happiness be used by a person who has used a Box before?"

O replies without any particular change in expression. "They cannot use the same Box, but if it's a different one, then yes. However, I do not use Boxes on the same subject twice."

If so, then I guess I can get Yanagi or Mogi to take some Misbegotten Happiness.

Now how do I go about doing that—?

★   ★   ★

"......Ngh."

My mind suddenly slows to a crawl. My brain is finally worn out. My head is in pain; I'm cracking under the influx of information. I can absorb and understand only so many insane revelations without my mind shutting down, and I've had about all I can take.

I look at my wristwatch. Not even a minute left before I'm in the theater.

"O."

There's still one thing I just have to check, though.

It's been on my mind this entire time, something I've been meaning to ask O the next time I encountered her after I realized her identity.

"What is it?"

Depending on the answer, my resolve may be shattered. This question is that crucial.

"The Misbegotten Happiness is an external-type Box, correct?"

There are internal- and external-type Boxes, categorized based on whether the owner believes its effects can actually be implemented in the real world.

Let's say the Misbegotten Happiness is an internal-type Box, and Aya didn't believe. It depends on the Box's level, but internal-type Boxes generally don't influence reality. In other words, all the bizarre, Box-induced incidents like the Rejecting Classroom, the Week in the Mud, and the Game of Indolence were part of the unreality within the Misbegotten Happiness. All these stories would be treated as vivid dreams of Aya's.

The same would go for Crime, Punishment, and the Shadow of Crime, too, of course.

I can't let this end with something so ridiculous. I wouldn't be able to bear it.

If the Misbegotten Happiness is not an external-type Box, then everything I have done will be rendered meaningless.

"Yes, it's an external-type, and a level ten. Her faith in her ability to make others happy is almost flawless. Your worries are unfounded, so relax."

Judging by her tone, it's the truth.

Whew, that was close.

Everything that's happened wasn't a lie.

My plan to strengthen the moral perspective of all humanity, the dog-people I created to judge the criminals who escaped justice, the excruciating agony I bore from the shadows of crime, Iroha Shindo's breakdown at my hands, Koudai Kamiuchi's death at my hands, and all the people I've warped with Crime, Punishment, and the Shadow of Crime—they were all real.

I'm relieved... Or I should be.

The truth is, as an owner, I do possess a vague sense of whether a Box is an internal or external type. The reason I still have to make sure is that I'm not the kind of person who can place much trust in hunches. Plus, given how crucial of an issue it is, I just needed proof.

All right, maybe I'll ask about one more important thing.

When I learned that Kazu's power came from the Misbegotten Happiness, a new question rose to my mind, one I had to ask.

"Kazu crushes Boxes, right?"

"That's what I've been saying."

"All of us were able to become owners because we liked the idea of Boxes and accepted them. But someone who crushes Boxes would be the complete opposite."

O listens to my question with that same pleasant and graceful smile.

"Would someone who rejects Boxes to such an extent ever be able to become an owner?"

O answers my question concisely.

"They would not."

I can't even remember how many times it's been now, but I'm teleported immediately after this conversation.

I'm seated in front of the screen.

In five minutes, the final movie, *15 Years Old and Earrings*, will play.

The audience consists of the decorative audience who look as if they're wearing masks of themselves. More of these unsmiling dolls are familiar faces than before. Behind and to my right is a realistic Yuri Yanagi. Aya

Otonashi is back and to the left. O-in-Iroha-Shindo's-form is nowhere to be seen.

After that, there's that odd phenomenon unique to this Box. A pitch-black hole, in the shape of someone sitting. An utter darkness that is now just two seats away—the abyss.

And then, next to me—

"Yeah."

It makes sense.

Kazu can't become an owner. He couldn't come up with the Silver Screen of Broken Wishes. He never could have made a Box with the lone purpose of stamping out my wish.

Who, then, is the owner?

Who could think only of me?

Who could wish only for me?

Only one person.

And so, sitting next to me is the star of this movie.

——Kokone Kirino.

The air-conditioning is too strong. It feels as if the unnaturally pure air is boring holes in my skin. I touch my earrings. I put holes in myself every chance I get, but it really isn't enough. I don't have nearly enough openings.

Kokone.

No matter how many holes I punch in my body, you won't get out. Seeing you there brings it all back from the distant past. That warmth in my arms never leaves. The once-gentle aura around us, the heat for us and only us, clashes sharply with reality to create a screeching that nearly drives me insane.

There's no way I can watch this movie to the end.

My mind will probably snap before the credits roll.

Why—

Why——

Why———

Why did it end up like this?

The Box I've been fighting belongs to Kokone? Does that mean I'm fighting her?

No.

It's not that we're fighting. Something doesn't fit.

If so, then who am I fighting?

What am I fighting?

What would it take for us to be happy?

No.

That thought is wrong.

I didn't choose happiness. I chose justice.

That's why this was a foregone conclusion.

This story was always going to end in tragedy.

Well, my psyche will crumble soon, I think. I'll probably be destroyed. But I'm fine with that. I have no problem with it. If I only figure out what is just and act to make it happen, I'll be able to work on autopilot. Empty-headed. No problem.

I know. I know what this is.

It's despair.

But despair already won a long time ago.

Yeah.

The screen flashes white, and then the light is red. It's the end of the world. I've seen it before.

What's about to appear on-screen is just another romantic drama with naive middle schoolers. I'm sure it'll be great. A guaranteed tearjerker. Everyone loves those, right? Stories about other people's suffering. Stories that make you cry over how very sad those poor characters are, and then you feel better. So please eat some popcorn and enjoy.

Everyone, a round of applause.

Clap.

Clap.

Clap.

Clap, clap.

◇◇◇ Kazuki Hoshino 09/11 FRI 10:31 PM ◇◇◇

Mogi still can't operate her wheelchair on her own.

That's why the one who brought her here, the one who called out "Found youuu," is not Mogi.

"Eh-heh-heh. Lucky me."

The person pushing Mogi in her wheelchair is a seemingly ordinary young girl.

That ordinary impression lasts only for a second, though. The only reason I thought it at all was because of her plain black bob and the prim dark-blue sailor uniform identifying her as an average middle schooler. But upon seeing her eyes, I can tell that this girl isn't going to act like one.

We're on a backstreet with not much foot traffic. The girl's pupils glimmer with so much fire beneath the glow of the streetlamp that I wonder if they forgot how to reflect light properly. It's as if they're made of aluminum foil.

They aren't normal.

"I found you. Kazuki Hoshino, Kazuki Hoshino, Kazuki Hoshino."

Full of energy, she twirls around on the spot. Just as I start to realize what's going on, she suddenly falls silent, biting her lip and fixing me with a glare.

"Lord Daiya's enemy."

I had a feeling that was it. This girl is one of the Daiya fanatics Yuri mentioned briefly.

"Hoshino..."

For some reason, this fanatic has brought Mogi with her.

"Mogi... What's going on...?"

Mogi is as white as a sheet and still in her pajamas, suggesting she was brought here against her will.

"Sh-she suddenly showed up and took me with her... I was really scared, but...it's not like I could fight back."

True. Mogi's body is in no state to do anything.

So what this girl is doing—no, what Daiya is doing—is the work of an undeniable coward.

"I had no idea what was going on. She took me outside, stole my cell phone, and then started trying to get in touch with you. That's when I realized why she came to get me."

"And then you found me the moment my phone rang...meaning we happened to be nearby..."

This road is close to the hospital. While it's unfortunate we were found so quickly, I probably would have responded to any contact from Mogi. This girl with her aluminum-foil eyes would have caught us sooner or later.

The girl begins to caress Mogi's hands.

Then she says:

"I'm going to break them now."

"Huh?" The word "break" has nothing to do with this situation. I don't get it.

"Fingers. Hers. I'm going to break them. I'm sorry."

Mogi's eyes go wide, and she looks up at the girl.

Unsure of how to respond, I decide to start by asking the first question that came to mind. "Wh-why would you do that?"

"Um...because that's the Order. From Lord Daiya."

"Hold up," Haruaki interrupts after watching us. "What would that accomplish?"

"Accomplish? I just said it's an Order, right?"

"That's not what I mean! What's the goal? Doesn't Daiya Oomine want something from Kazuki Hoshino?!"

"Oh yeah. Yeah, yeah. I was told to make Kazuki Hoshino come into the Silver Screen of Broken Wishes."

The girl replies as if the objective doesn't matter to her in the slightest.

For a fanatic of Daiya's like herself, maybe she doesn't care about the ends or the means. She simply obeys the instructions given to her. She doesn't prioritize, either.

"Don't you feel anything seeing Kasumi in this state? You're just fine doing this?" Haruaki is a little stunned by her behavior, but he lays into her anyway.

Upon hearing this, the girl tilts her head all the way to the side, leaning over Mogi and staring at her upside down. Mogi squeaks at suddenly finding that face looking at her.

"I feel bad for her." It's an unexpected reply. "But I feel even worse for myself."

"Wh-why?"

She raises her head again and mutters, "I have AIDS, you know? I'm gonna die eventually. Yeah. I'm worse off."

But her tone makes it sound as if she doesn't care at all.

"So does my pity mean anything?"

She doesn't care. For this girl, "feeling bad" for Mogi is yet another thing that doesn't matter to her.

Nothing matters except her devotion to Daiya.

That is abnormal.

It's so abnormal that Haruaki is too stunned to reply.

I'm sure of it. This girl will indeed snap Mogi's fingers one by one without batting an eye. She'll do it without any deep feelings or thought to what it means.

".........Ugh." I let out a sigh, then laugh scornfully. "C'mon, man."

Daiya, what are you even doing?

Is this what you want? I thought you couldn't stand people with no imagination? Isn't this girl here exactly what you described?

"What's so funny?"

The girl stares at me angrily with those aluminum-foil eyes.

Should I be afraid of those eyes?

I don't really think so.

In fact, I'm convinced they're a hindrance.

A hindrance to her that means I don't need to hold back at all.

Here's the thing about people with no imagination, people who just do what they're told. From a certain perspective, such a total lack of original thought—

"Huh? Oh!"

—leaves them wide-open.

The girl gives a cry of confusion when I abruptly dash forward. But she can't think, so she can't react.

I weave around behind her.

"Ah, ngh!"

I squeeze her neck with both hands.

The girl lets go of the wheelchair without thinking.

"Haruaki!"

He's been watching me in wide-eyed surprise, but he knows exactly why I called out to him.

Now that the wheelchair is out of the girl's hands, he snatches it away.

"*Koff, koff!*"

Not loosening my grip on the coughing girl, I seize her by the collar and then push her down without giving her a chance to respond.

The girl's aluminum-foil eyes are now full of shock. I can see the beginnings of rising fear.

Who gives a crap, though? It's worth no more than dog food.

"Not having any doubts is a strength, but still."

I ready my right hand.

Then I plunge it into her chest like a sword.

"Agh, guh!"

"This is what happens if you don't have any will or determination."

I pull out the mass-produced offshoot of Crime, Punishment, and the Shadow of Crime.

"Ah..."

The girl looks at what I have in my hand: an inferior Box that resembles a black bean.

"S-stop! M-my link! My link to Lord Daiya will go away!" she shrieks desperately.

I snort in amusement. "You never had one to begin with. Just shut up."

I'm taking back Maria, and I'll do whatever it takes to anyone who gets in my way.

I crush it.

—*Crsssh.*

There isn't much resistance. It feels like squishing a pill bug.

"Aaaaaaaaaaaaaaaaaaaaaaaaaaaaaaaaaaaaaaaaaaaaaaaaaaaaaaaaaaaaaaaa aaaaaaaaaaaaaaaaaaaaaaaaaaaaaaaaaaaaaaaaaaaaaaaaaaaaaaaaaaaaaaaah!"

The girl faints, just as Iroha did when I destroyed her Box.

".........Whew."

It doesn't make me feel much of anything.

I just did what I could. That's all.

Looking down at the girl where she has collapsed, I stand and brush the dirt off my clothes. When I glance at Haruaki, I find he's been watching me with round eyes.

"......What's wrong, Haruaki?"

"...Uh, well...it's just that you did something weird."

"Yeah, I've gained the ability to remove and destroy Boxes."

"Oh...okay..."

Despite my explanation, Haruaki's expression is still dubious.

"...? It looks like you have something else to say."

"Oh yeah. Um...man, you don't pull your punches."

"Pull my punches? Why would I need to do that? She was going to break Mogi's fingers, wasn't she? You could tell she had no qualms about it, right?"

"Y-yeah. What you did, yeah, it was justified."

Justified.

Yes, it was justified.

So Haruaki's confusion is a little bewildering.

More important is Mogi, now that she's suddenly involved. I lean over and smile at her in her wheelchair.

"Are you okay?"

"Th-thanks."

I thought I spoke to her kindly, but she still seems bemused.

"......"

...Now I know I need to take care. My actions are a little bit strange.

Mercy was a luxury I couldn't afford, though... As I look at Mogi and try to justify my actions in my mind, I suddenly spot something.

"Huh? Mogi? Are you hiding something in your left pocket?" I ask, pointing it out.

"Ulp." Mogi won't look me in the eye.

What's with that reaction?

What is it? I'm about to ask, when Haruaki taps me on the shoulder.

"Bad news, Hosshi. Looks like that scream got everyone's attention," he tells me.

Lights have appeared in the doorways of houses nearby, and a commotion is beginning.

It makes sense. This place doesn't see a lot of traffic, but it's not deserted like that tunnel under the tracks that Iroha brought me to. This girl was really reckless for trying to hurt someone in a place like this.

"What should we do? I don't want to take the time to explain the situation."

"I'm worried about her, but let's get out of here. She's down for the count, so people may get the wrong idea and think we hurt her. Maybe we should lean her against that wall over there. Someone will probably hand her over to the police."

I nod and do as Haruaki says.

We beat a hasty retreat, and once we've got some distance, we begin walking over to Kokone's again.

But there's a problem, and I shouldn't even have to say it's Mogi.

Mogi has no idea what any of this is about. I can't tell her about Boxes and drag her into this.

If Daiya is going to keep giving Orders that involve Mogi, though, then I can't just take her back to the hospital and be done with it. There's no telling if a similar incident might happen again.

Maybe I should explain just a bit of what's going on to her? And is it the right thing to do, to take someone who can't move freely?

"Mogi, what do you wanna do?"

Unable to decide myself, I instinctively ask the person in question. Clueless about the situation as she is, there's no way she can make a good call, but still.

As Haruaki pushes her wheelchair along, Mogi doesn't answer right away. Then she says with a troubled look, "What would be the best course of action?"

It sounds like a throwaway response. But it bothers me.

I mean, that's definitely not a natural reply. Normally, wouldn't someone ask what's going on or just be lost before they got to that?

"Mogi, I'm sorry!"

"Huh? Oh!"

I can't stop wondering about what's hidden in her shirt.

I shove my hand into her pocket, and it touches something hard. Mogi's face has gone bright red in either panic or discomfort over being touched, and she protests weakly. She doesn't have much strength, though, so I take the hard little object with ease.

It's—

"A stun gun...?"

Why? Why would Mogi be carrying this? Would she have had the time to hide this in her pocket when Daiya's fanatic took her from the hospital? Did Mogi always have a stun gun with her there?

My conclusion is only natural.

Mogi had that stun gun beforehand.

In other words—

—she knew that the fanatic was going to attack her.

"......"

Then there's the thing I discovered when I touched her.

As the one with the "Empty Box," I had to notice this, at least.

—Mogi is an owner.

—Mogi is a Subject.

If she knew she was going to be attacked, then why didn't she use the stun gun when it happened? Who did she plan to use it on, then?

What Order has she received from Daiya? If Daiya has given her an Order, then who would her target be...?

"I didn't want to tell you," Mogi says in a small voice. "I didn't want to tell you I had remembered about Boxes. After all—"

She grabs on to my sleeve with her shaky strength.

"*—I remembered I gave up on you.*"

"Huh?"

That was not what I expected her to say.

Given that she's a Subject, I had thought she had been ordered by Daiya to attack me.

But when I really, really think about it, using Mogi for that would be more trouble than it was worth for Daiya. So the reason why Mogi is being so uncomfortable is...

"I remembered the Rejecting Classroom," Mogi tells me sadly.

Yes, because I found out she recalled those days of hopelessness.

"That said, my memories of what actually happened aren't clear at all. I think it's because my memory was a foggy mess from the time I was in the Rejecting Classroom."

That's a small mercy, at least. If she had remembered everything, she might not have even been able to speak with me as she is now.

"I'm positive I caused you and Otonashi a lot of trouble, though. I get that feeling. And—"

Mogi lets go of my arm and says, with a smile that takes all her effort, "The memory of you dumping me is crystal clear."

Yeah, our romantic relationship…ended back then.

It was over.

We spent a life's worth of time putting an end to it.

There is no undoing that, not ever.

And yet, in my regret, I saved the photo of Mogi's sunflower smile. That was a mistake. I was just unable to take responsibility for my actions.

"But that doesn't change anything, see? You always have been, and always will be, my hope. That's still the same," she tells me.

The look on Mogi's face seems cheerful.

Does she accept it? But even if she does, that doesn't mean I can keep my mouth shut. There are so many things I need to tell her.

But Mogi being Mogi, she doesn't give me that chance.

"Okay. Let's not talk about me now. Let's talk about what happens next."

"Hold on; it's just—"

"Oomine intends to make Otonashi lose her memory."

"——!!"

Everything I was going to say to Mogi is scattered to the wind.

I'm so sorry, but you're right. That's the top priority; we have to talk about it.

After all—that would be the final nail in my coffin.

What I'm trying to do here isn't just to destroy Maria's Misbegotten Happiness. It's to convince Maria to give up the Misbegotten Happiness herself.

If Maria's memory is taken away, though, I'll never be able to get through to her. For Maria, I might as well be a stranger if she can't remember. To make matters worse, she's so stubborn. She'll never listen to me if I'm a stranger.

Losing all recollection of me—would pretty much render me powerless.

But how would she do it? ...No, that's easy. Just use the Misbegotten Happiness on someone I know. Maria's said before that that would erase her memory.

"Grr, Daiya...!"

I should've expected as much. Even when he's on his last leg, he can still hit me right where it hurts.

"Mogi." I'm grinding my teeth, but the conversation still needs to move forward. "How did you get this information?" I ask.

"You know I received Crime, Punishment, and the Shadow of Crime, right?"

"Yeah."

"I got an Order a little while ago."

"What was it?"

"It said I should brace myself because a fanatic might be coming for me. Also that I should get in touch with you."

So Mogi had been packing a stun gun because she knew an attack was on the way. I guess the reason she didn't use it earlier was because she realized the attacker was taking her phone to make contact with me, so she just let it all unfold.

"And you were trying to get ahold of me so you could tell me Daiya was going to make Maria lose her memories?"

"That's right."

That made sense. I understood that part, but...

"Hold on a second. Why would Daiya do that? Why would he have to reveal his plans?"

"Huh?"

Mogi's reaction alerts me to something.

That's it. Of course it is. There is no reason Daiya would do that.

So the one who made that Order—is another Ruler.

But the only person besides Daiya with the abilities of a Ruler was Iroha.

I can't imagine him yielding that kind of power to anyone other than her. Iroha said she was the only one, too.

"—Still."

Still, if it's Iroha we're dealing with, there is one person she might have passed along that power to in secret.

A person she can trust, who would use that ability skillfully and who possessed the good judgment to stop her if it came down to it.

I say her name: "*Yuri.*"

Mogi looks confused. "...Um?"

I was pretty confident in my reasoning, but I must have made an error along the way.

"Oh...guess not."

"You're not wrong."

"Hmm?"

"But why do you call me by my last name 'Mogi' and Yanagi by 'Yuri'?"

"......"

Huh?

"Does that bug you?"

"O-of course it does!" Mogi retorts, blushing.

I guess my only error was assuming I made an error.

"...Um."

At any rate, it really was Yuri who sent Mogi that Order. Her intent was to let me know what's happening on her end through Mogi.

Sending her to Daiya is turning out to be a very good choice.

But...

...at the same time, her presence could create a problem.

Daiya could use *Yuri* to remove all traces of me from Maria's mind.

"Hosshi, what should we do? The game has changed a lot. My plan to hide won't do us much good now, will it?" Haruaki says.

I nod. "Even if we do lie low, there's no avoiding ultimatums from Daiya anymore."

"Right."

"Daiya will probably be pulling out all the stops with his Orders, too. He can even use mass media, after all."

Haruaki goes quiet, maybe envisioning the dog-woman on TV.

"We managed to escape earlier, but his crazed followers are also a danger. I never would have thought people would have so much blind faith in him. If these fanatics learn that Daiya will lose the power of Crime, Punishment, and the Shadow of Crime, they may do something crazy even without an Order."

"Ngh. So what do we do?"

There's one answer.

"I have to go into the Silver Screen of Broken Wishes."

If possible, I had wanted to wait it out and let it end that way.

If I go into the Silver Screen of Broken Wishes, it means I'll be using the power of the Empty Box on Daiya and obliterating Crime, Punishment, and the Shadow of Crime. In short, exercising the power to crush a Box in front of Maria.

Truth be told, I want to avoid showing my ability to her.

Let's be real—can I actually talk her into casting aside her Box when she knows I'm capable of smashing it? It'd be like trying to persuade her while making a threat at the same time. Like clutching a knife and saying, *I'm not going to do anything, so you stab yourself.*

Maria and I have parted ways completely, I know. But if I do this, it would only make the situation even worse.

Nevertheless, I have no other choice.

If I tough it out in the real world without going into the Silver Screen of Broken Wishes, and Maria's memory gets wiped using Yuri, then it'll be game over.

I stare angrily into the palms of my hands.

No matter many times I look, my palms are completely unremarkable, much smaller than Haruaki's.

But they hold the power, the hubris to crush wishes.

"I'll defeat Daiya with these hands."

I clench my fists.

Haruaki watches me and gives a small nod. "I see—so you're going to him," he says, then focuses on some point in the distance. It's as if he's mulling over something, or he's unsure of something. "I wanna make a request."

The far-off gaze shifts steadily to me.

"Take me and Kiri with you."

Haruaki lowers his head.

And that's not all he's doing, I soon find out, as he falls to his knees and bows on the ground in front of me.

"H-Haruaki!"

"Please!" he shouts, head pressed to the ground. "I want to save Daiyan. And if it's even possible, I think Kiri is the only one who can do it. Their relationship is broken beyond repair, and it'll hurt both of them, I know. But... But I think Kiri's the only one who can do something for Daiyan."

He lifts his head. Haruaki's eyes are slightly moist with tears.

"I want to help them work it out somehow! Even if it doesn't go well, I know I want to be there with them at the end."

Anyone could tell that it's a sincere request.

All the same, I can't answer right away.

After all, I have to consider the complications it might bring. When it comes down to it, my top priority is Maria.

My lack of sympathy does bother me. But I'm Maria's knight.

"Hoshino..."

For that reason, when Mogi says my name, I expect an accusation.

She doesn't look accusatory, though. Her face has gone white.

"...What's wrong?"

"U-um, I got an Order from Yuri."

Then Mogi tells me:

"She says Otonashi became a Subject."

15 Years Old and Earrings, SCENE 4, 2/3

11. A PARK - NOON

A big park with a pitcher's mound. Though the chatter of children can be heard in the distance, there is no one around Daiya and Kokone.
On the mound is a black-haired Daiya. Kokone, wearing glasses, stands atop home base with the wall to her rear.
Behind the park spreads a field of wheat, glittering gold.

                    DAIYA
          Here.

Daiya tosses an easy curveball. Kokone stands ready for it, visibly flustered. She accidentally hits the ball with her glove, sending it rolling away. She scoops it up hurriedly, and when she throws it back, it doesn't reach Daiya.
The two of them repeat the same sequence several times.

                    DAIYA
          You suck.

Daiya speaks with a laugh as he retrieves a wayward ball.

> KOKONE
> Ohhh! I'm sorry!

Kokone somehow manages to catch the ball when she holds out the glove and supports it with both hands. Her return toss still falls short.

> KOKONE
> Daiya… Don't you get bored playing catch with me…?

> DAIYA
> Well, I definitely can't call it practice.

He snatches up the rolling ball.

> DAIYA
> But I don't mind.

> KOKONE
> I can't even get the ball to you, though. All my throws are way off.

Kokone sends the ball in the wrong direction yet again. Daiya chases after it.

> DAIYA
> Throw it wherever you want.

He calmly picks up the ball.

> DAIYA
> I'll go get it every time.

Smiling, Daiya is truly okay with the arrangement. Kokone, on the other hand, doesn't like relying on him like that, so she runs up to Daiya to get some pointers on how to throw.

She spends a while intently learning how to move her arms and space her legs. Daiya seems to enjoy this, too.

                        KOKONE
        Okay, here goes.

She is able to throw the ball several times with
somewhat better form. She's getting better and better as time passes.

                        KOKONE
        Here!

The ball goes straight into Daiya's glove.

                        DAIYA
        You got it to me.

Daiya grins.

                        KOKONE
        I did.

Kokone grins.

            12. THE PARK — A WINTER NIGHT

Daiya, his hair colored and a single piercing in
his right ear, is throwing the ball at a concrete
wall by himself like a man possessed. The ball bangs
loudly against the wall, over and over. There is no
one to catch it.
    The stalks of wheat have been harvested, leaving
the field barren.

                        DAIYA
        ......Huff......huff......

He throws with a wide swing. The powerful pitch
shoots upward, jamming itself into the net above
the concrete with a crash. It remains stuck there
instead of falling down.
    It's impossible to retrieve.
    Daiya glares at the ball for a time.

```
                      DAIYA (VO)
        Purity is…

                      DAIYA (VO)
        …beautiful…

                      DAIYA (VO)
        …and delicate.

                      DAIYA (VO)
        Once it's lost, no one can ever get it back.
```

◆◆◆ Daiya Oomine 09/11 FRI 10:50 PM ◆◆◆

I can't take any more.

For some reason, my head keeps ringing with a sound like the alarms announcing an incoming earthquake.

On-screen is Kokone Kirino, back when she had black hair. Then there's me, mild mannered and polite, not questioning the world at all.

I knew it.

I knew this would happen if I saw *15 Years Old and Earrings*, starring Kokone Kirino.

But that forewarning does nothing to stop the pain.

"——Ah."

Malice.

Malice.

—Malice.

It feels as if I'm pinned to the seat of the theater by a blade of animus. Everything has changed color since then. Anyone can see the murky hue that's joined the others: the truth. It feels like viscous mud, as if everything is working against me.

This malice that I should have grown accustomed to gnaws away at me.

Seeing the past beauty of the world forces me to see how different it is today—the impurity.

Yes.

I just wish I could pass out right now.

I just wish I could be at ease right now.

"Lord Daiya."

A voice yanks my consciousness back, calling my name with that pompous, unpleasant title attached.

Resisting the lethargy unique to the Silver Screen of Broken Wishes, I summon my strength and turn my head toward the source of the voice. An older woman I don't recognize is near the entrance to the theater. With my head hazy from the Box's assault, I wonder who she is for a moment, but I soon identify her. Though I don't really recognize her face, the fact that she addressed me by that title means she must be one of my fanatical Subjects.

The one here now is a different devotee from the middle school girl I met in Shinjuku. She wasn't my only crazed follower. I remember now. The woman walking toward me now is a university student who repeatedly tried to take her own life. A woman who mistook my Crime, Punishment, and the Shadow of Crime for a spiritual experience.

Ironically enough, the presence of someone less-than-innocent relaxes me.

It's probably because she helps me feel the reality I know and not the warmth found in that movie. It's hilarious that something unpleasant makes me feel better.

"What is it?"

Once I pull myself together through the headache and the nausea, I remember what role this fanatic was assigned. She was given the task of keeping an eye on Kazu's actions.

I gave that middle schooler an Order to use Mogi to deliver an ultimatum to Kazu and make him come here, and that I didn't care if she broke Mogi's fingers. At the same time, I ordered this college girl to go along with her in secret to observe how things went down. I figured Kazu and crew would be so fixated on the fanatic with Mogi that they wouldn't notice my other Subject.

I then gave her an Order to come report back to me here in the Silver Screen of Broken Wishes after she had witnessed everything.

The college girl comes up next to me and kneels down like a vassal about to swear her fealty to me.

Her expression is quite panicked.

I can guess what it means.

"Did the threat with Mogi fail?"

"Yes."

Since he has the power to crush Boxes, the answer is about what I expected. I made that Order before I heard what O had to say. Kazu's ability pretty much leaves that scheme dead in the water.

I was not expecting what the woman says next, however.

"But that's not all. Our plans have been leaked to them!"

I can't process that situation straightaway. I scowl.

"What do you mean? How much has been leaked?"

"They've heard that my lord's goal is to make Aya Otonashi lose her memory!"

"What?"

How did this happen?

It goes without saying, but I've mentioned that here, within the Silver Screen of Broken Wishes. There's no way it could have leaked to the outside.

"Would O be able to relay that to them? ...No, I really can't imagine that now that she's said Kazu is her enemy. If so, then—"

"Forgive the intrusion, but I can tell you that. It was Kasumi Mogi who told them."

"Mogi?"

Can Mogi tell what's going on in here? How could she?

After a little thought, I quickly arrive at the answer and turn back and to my right.

To the culprit behind the leak.

To a girl I had already considered released from duty.

"Yuri Yanagi."

"Huh? What is it?"

Yanagi's eyes open wide, as if she has absolutely no idea why I would be suddenly calling her name. But I'm familiar with her theatrics by now.

"Shindo gave you just a bit of her power, huh? Without my permission."

That's the situation as I read it.

Yanagi drops the clueless look in favor of a bright smile.

"Eh-heh-heh." Her expression then turns cold and hard. "So the jig is up. You're right. And Kasumi is my sole Subject." She's being awfully brazen after her innocent performance just a moment ago.

Yanagi's defiance prompts my crazed university student follower to glare at her with unbridled hostility. I motion for her to stand down with a hand, then continue my conversation with Yanagi.

"Did you forget that my success would have benefitted you and Kazu?"

"Oh? I had no idea. I said this before, but do you think anyone would obey someone who murdered them? You believe you can make women do whatever you want. It's disgusting. You should just die."

She's useless.

With my power, I could work up her shadow of a crime and put her through a world of pain. She's my Subject; I can control her actions as much as I want.

And yet, she's still letting her emotions control her.

I wait for Yanagi's mouth to open, knowing that as soon as she finishes talking, I'm going to give her shadow of a crime hell.

But—

"*Just kidding.*"

—Yanagi grins.

"What?"

"I said, just kidding, Oomine. Please don't be angry. It's not what you think. I'm actually helping you."

I have no doubt her words are misleading. I know that, but I decide not to mess with her shadow of a crime just yet and instead question her true intent.

"You're trying to say that leaking my plans is helping me?"

It sounds like a pathetic excuse and nothing more.

But Yanagi is brimming with self-assurance as she declares, "That's right."

What's up with her attitude?

Yanagi is smart. Surely she must be self-aware enough to know that, as one of my Subjects, she pretty much has a knife held to her throat. Maybe she's just confident I won't use the knife?

"Please just imagine Kazuki's reaction when he finds out you plan to wipe Otonashi's memory."

I finally piece together what Yanagi is saying.

"Maybe this is what you're getting at. You did it…"

I say it.

"…to draw Kazuki into the Silver Screen of Broken Wishes."

She nods slowly, and a little arrogantly. "Exactly. Don't you think that's the most reliable way of getting him to do what you want? There's no need to be terrible and break Kasumi's fingers."

I had attempted to use Mogi in a now-meaningless countermeasure against O. It's understandable that Yanagi would find the threat ineffectual.

"Hey, Otonashi. It'll bring Kazuki here, right?"

She's even going to the trouble of getting confirmation from Aya.

Aya's been watching us almost like a bystander, but now that she has to join the conversation, she replies, "…Yeah, it almost certainly will."

If she's saying he'll show, then there's pretty much no doubt.

"See? I have helped you."

Kazu is on his way here thanks to Yanagi.

I'm going to come face-to-face with him.

Dammit…

I consider what Yanagi has done.

Damn her. She has really done it now.

It's not that I hadn't given any thought to baiting him with a threat to purge Otonashi's memories. I did understand that it was a viable option to draw him to me.

Why should I have to take on such a risk, though?

If Kazu knows what I'm cooking up beforehand, then naturally, he's going to take countermeasures. It raises the chance of my strategy failing. What's worse, he has the extremely formidable power to obliterate Boxes.

If Yanagi wanted to act in my best interests, I would have wanted her to put together some completely different threat to tell Mogi.

Still, I'm surprised she'd go to such lengths to split Otonashi and Kazu apart...

"Kazu is probably gonna hate you when he finds out what you've done."

"No he won't. What're you talking about?" Yanagi says with a matter-of-fact look. "I tried to keep you from harming Mogi and exposed your schemes, right? I did everything I could for Kazuki. In fact, I think he'll be so grateful, he couldn't hate me, don't you think?"

...What is she on about?

But now that I think about it... No, she's right.

From Kazu's point of view, divulging my plans will just look like a helping hand. And she did protect Mogi, too. This girl is playing the role Kazu wants to a T.

She's hanging on to her position to the bitter end.

"And you call this help for me..."

On top of it all, she's covering her own ass, too. Now that he's aware my thrust is to make Aya forget him, Kazu has probably surmised that Yanagi will be the target of the Misbegotten Happiness. And of course, once he's got that down, he'll think of a means of stopping that—a means of protecting Yanagi.

And thus, she raises her own chances of making it through this.

"—I'm sure you think it is, Yanagi, but you've dug your own grave."

"Huh?"

Yanagi's eyes go wide, and I seize her shadow of a crime.

"——A-ahhh!!"

She is experiencing the murders she committed in the Game of Indolence.

"Aaaaaaaaaaaaaaaaaaaaaahhh! Aaaaaaaaaaaaaaaaaaaaaaaaaaaaaaaaaaaahhh!!"

She doesn't stand a chance of enduring it.

"Before, I thought I would need Otonashi to use the Misbegotten Happiness in front of Kazu to make it really sink in that she's forgotten about him. But if he already knows I'm going to make her erase her memory, if he's on his way here now, that changes everything. He'll know what happened if her memories are long gone by the time he arrives. When he sees that, it will break him."

Yanagi tumbles out of her seat.

"Aaaaaaaaaaaaaaaaaaaaaaaaaaaaaaaaaaaaaaaaaaaaaaaaaaaaaaaaaaaaaaa aaaaaaaaaaaaaaaaaaaaaaaaaaaaaaaaaaaaaaaaaaaaaaaaaaaaaaaaaaaahhh!!"

"You've destroyed yourself and Kazu with your own actions. Congratulations. Now, despair and beg for the Misbegotten Happiness."

The crime is murder.

Yanagi may be sly, but her heart is good-natured. Pure. She is far from being a villain. She doesn't stand a chance under the weight of all her sins.

And yet—

".........I won't."

I frown at that small, rasping voice.

"I won't. If I did, it would mean I lost to the Game of Indolence. I know I'm despicable. But I had no choice. I had to do those things for my own survival. Whether it was good or bad doesn't matter; if I couldn't have done anything else, I have to accept that fact."

"Oh, shut up, murderer."

"*You* shut up! I won't let it go to waste. Kazuki came to see me at home so many times. He helped me to understand that I did only what I had to do. He forgave all the bad stuff I did. So no matter how much I suffer, I won't let my guilt win... I won't!"

"...I wonder how long you can keep that up?"

She talks big, but there's no way she can hold out for long. I'll just keep at her until she begs for someone to save her.

But...

"Stop, Oomine!" Aya says in a still voice. "I won't use the Misbegotten Happiness this way, not even if she asks for it herself."

I release my grip on the shadow of a crime at her words.

"Don't ever try to force someone into asking for the Misbegotten Happiness again. I've made up my mind. Even if you torture someone to make them ask for it, I will never use it."

If Aya says she won't, then it's a safe bet.

So Yanagi is released from her torment.

"Unh, ahhh...ahhh......" As tears stream down her face, she fixes an angry gaze on me. "...Eh, heh-heh...sounds like she isn't going to do it... You're pathetic."

Crawling up into her seat, Yanagi lies there motionless as if utterly exhausted.

"Kazuki...," she whispers. Calling the name of her absent crush? Regardless, her behavior makes it apparent she really did relay the situation to Kazu through Mogi in order to hinder me.

"Tch, you stupid bitch..."

The whole thing probably would've worked if I'd been able to wrangle her, so that's a one-in-a-million chance that I missed.

...That, or maybe it's Kazu's fault again that she was able to stick it out. Maybe it was due to his patience in facing down the Game of Indolence and helping Yanagi recover?

Exhaustion washes over me in a wave, and I fall roughly into my seat.

The kneeling fanatic has been watching me uneasily. It's unpleasant.

"Leave."

"Huh?"

"I don't want to even see you."

She seems about to say something, but a fanatic isn't going to talk back. As instructed, she disappears from the theater.

"_____"

The movie is proceeding at a steady pace.

The scene where Rino burns Kiri with the cigarettes should be starting pretty soon.

At any rate, the playing field has changed yet again thanks to Yanagi. The headache is worse, the nausea is worse, and my strength is spent, but I still have to review the current status quo.

Sitting in my theater seat, I cradle my head in my hands and think.

The situation has changed dramatically since the end of *Repeat, Reset, Reset.*

I have identified five major differences.

*   *   *

—O is no longer Kazu's ally.

—Kazu has gained the power to crush Boxes.

—I've figured out the owner is Kokone Kirino.

—Kazu is coming into the Silver Screen of Broken Wishes.

—Aya will not use the Misbegotten Happiness if I use Crime, Punishment, and the Shadow of Crime to make them desperate.

These all change my conclusion. I had been thinking I could win if I could make Kazu give up. If he lost hope, he would hand over the Silver Screen of Broken Wishes, too.

That was my mistake, though. Even if Kazu did throw in the towel, I would still lose as long as Kiri held on to the Silver Screen of Broken Wishes.

On the other hand, breaking Kazu is still essential. If he has the ability to crush Boxes, I have to neutralize that power.

Here are the conditions for victory:

1. Summon the owner—i.e., Kokone Kirino—here and destroy the Silver Screen of Broken Wishes before the end of September 11.
2. Shatter Kazu's will by making Aya use the Misbegotten Happiness, thus erasing her memory, before he can touch my chest.

What the hell? How am I supposed to accomplish all that?

For starters, how do I call Kiri here? And once I do call her here, how do I destroy her Box? How am I supposed to persuade Kiri when she's got a Box specifically created to crush my Crime, Punishment, and the Shadow of Crime? I can't see myself changing the mind of someone so determined in an hour and change. My only option is to find some way to destroy the Box by force.

But a way doesn't exist, though. It's impossible.

And while we're at it, how do I even get Aya to use the Misbegotten Happiness? At this rate, I'm going to have to call someone who both knows Kazu and has always needed the Misbegotten Happiness. And even if I do manage to get them here, they probably won't make the decision lightly. Kazu could destroy my Crime, Punishment, and the Shadow of Crime in the meantime. In any case, he can simply crush Boxes with just a touch to the chest.

It's impossible.

It's impossible for me to win as long as I can't control Aya Otonashi freely.

"............"

Wait.

Oh, is that what it comes down to?

There's one sole requirement for me to come out on top.

Namely—

—make Aya Otonashi into a Subject.

I have to use Kazu's Box-crushing power to do away with the Silver Screen of Broken Wishes. With Orders, I can even make someone commit suicide. If I tell Kazu that I'll Order Aya to kill herself unless he smashes Kiri's Box, he should have no choice but to do it.

What's more, I can also force Aya to use the Misbegotten Happiness with an Order. If I wipe Aya's memories in front of Kazu's eyes, he'll be a broken man.

I can meet both of my conditions for victory if Aya Otonashi becomes a Subject.

But here's the thing.

"I could never pull that off...," I mutter as I watch Kiri struggling desperately on the screen.

"Stop! Why are you doing this, Rino?!"

Aya Otonashi possesses a powerful will. There's no reason she should become a Subject. It's pointless to even think about it.

"Noooooooooooooooooooooooooooooooooooooo!!"

The life is being squeezed out of me. The cry from the speakers reaches my ears and tears away at my heart.

I try to touch my earrings, but even that is too much for me. Just extending my hand leaves me immobile with exhaustion.

★　　　★　　　★

Just end.
End.
End.
End.
End.
End everything.

"...Maybe..."
Maybe this is it?
Should I just give up?
Should I just give up trying to use my own body to realize my earnest wish?
"......Should I just kill them?"
Just kill Kazuki Hoshino.
And Kokone Kirino.
I can do it using my Subjects.
If I do, I'll be rid of both the Silver Screen of Broken Wishes and the power to crush Boxes.
I know. If I go through with it, my mind won't survive. My mind is already close to the brink as it is, so it would be shattered.
Either way, the fact of the matter is that I won't be whole for much longer anyway. I need to find someone to pass along my cause to. I need to grant the power of a Ruler to a person capable of wielding Crime, Punishment, and the Shadow of Crime the right way.
Shindo was defeated, though. She had seemed to have what it takes to inherit my will, albeit with some slight deviations, yet she is no longer able to use Crime, Punishment, and the Shadow of Crime.
Fanatics are no good, either. They're suited to following, not issuing orders from above. I try to conjure up some other faces, but no one who seems able to handle it correctly comes to mind.
No one has it in them to sacrifice themselves and act for the sake of the world.
They don't exist.

That kind of person—

That kind of hope—

Someone who can carry on my cause for me—

"_____

_____

_____exists."

One person.

One person, the only one I can imagine, might be even better suited to the task than I am.

The one who declared herself to be a Box and cast aside everything except for the pursuit of her mission.

Aya Otonashi.

I understand in a flash.

It feels ridiculous, like throwing a jigsaw puzzle without a single piece connected and somehow having it all come together perfectly. At any rate, it's all so clear now.

I stand up. I'm so weak that I can't even touch my earrings, but I don't have time for that. Defying the force of the Silver Screen of Broken Wishes, I face Aya.

I feel so awful that saying a single word might make me vomit blood. The vertigo throws off my sense of balance, and my field of vision is askew.

All the same, my mouth lifts into a smile.

"Aya, you've been searching for a Box all this time. That's why you've been pursuing O, pursuing owners. All so you can perfect your wish."

Aya's brows furrow, and she gives me a hard look.

"Everything, from your willingness to spend a lifetime in the Rejecting Classroom to the way you stuck with Kazu because O had taken a liking to him, has been so you can get ahold of a Box. You changed the entire trajectory of your life to reach this goal. Every bit of you is devoted to this mission."

"Yeah, that's right. What about it?"

The truth is, it's an exercise in futility. Aya cannot obtain her ideal Box. That's why she struggles on, ignorant of O's true nature.

What is misbegotten will remain misbegotten.

However, only if she has to fight on her own.

What if she met a person moving in the same direction?

What if she met a kindred spirit?

"You should be happy."

What if there just so happened to be someone in possession of a similar Box?

"Your heart's desire is about to come true."

I'm serious, and my earnestness reaches Aya as well. She gazes at me intensely.

"Where is it? Where is the Box I want?"

The Misbegotten Happiness and Crime, Punishment, and the Shadow of Crime are alike.

Boxes crafted of powerful emotions, yet somehow frail and cold, yet with an infinite capacity to mean more.

I have always felt they were similar.

"It's right here." I tap my chest. *"Crime, Punishment, and the Shadow of Crime is the Box you've been looking for."*

Yes, if she uses this, Aya can escape from this unfeeling, misbegotten quicksand.

Her wide-eyed gaze then lowers, and she shakes her head.

"Your imagination must have really gotten away from you. Your Crime, Punishment, and the Shadow of Crime is not the Box I need. A Box that victimizes others doesn't just conflict with my ideals—it's the polar opposite. What happened with Yanagi is the perfect example. You can't convince me otherwise."

"That's because I'm using it."

Aya regards me again.

"You're right that in my hands, this Box will result in some unfortunate losses for others, because this is how I'm trying to transform the world. But this power is more than the ability to create dog-people. Its original strength lies in control. No, that description paints it in a negative light. To phrase it in a way that's more amenable to you—"

I look into her eyes shining with will and tell her:

"—it's the power to lead."

Aya's gaze changes.

Yeah, I knew it. This Box is the one she's been searching for.

"It has what you want, too, of course."

I tell her with conviction.

"The power to lead others to happiness."

"It can't be—but, but……"

Though she can't accept it logically yet, Aya has seen it.

That what I'm telling her is the truth.

That the Box she has been seeking is here.

I begin walking over to Aya Otonashi.

Naturally, the Silver Screen of Broken Wishes is keeping me sluggish. And it's getting worse; now, with each step I make, the shadows of crime gnaw at me as if my very nerves are on fire. Unable to walk straight, I support myself against the seats as I make my way to the rear row where she is.

"—Heh-heh."

My body is in agony, but joy swells up in my heart.

After all, I've finally found my long-awaited solution.

From the moment I obtained the Box, I was prepared to fall because of using Crime, Punishment, and the Shadow of Crime. I braced myself for the possibility that I would go insane in the near future, flailing and thrashing until I met my pitiful end.

This Box came into being under the assumption that someone would pick up where I left off.

But who would that be?

Maybe I understood without even being conscious of it.

I mean, wasn't I aware that she was hope itself? I don't know; maybe it was due to my repeated interactions with her in the Rejecting Classroom, or maybe it didn't have anything to do with that and I simply understood her aloof nature. Either way, I'm sure I'd already identified someone capable of taking on this power when I obtained my Box.

If so, then Crime, Punishment, and the Shadow of Crime has always been—

*   *   *

—a Box meant to be given to Aya Otonashi.

"......*Huff, huff*..."
I reach Aya Otonashi's side.
Though she's a bit hesitant, I don't think she's going to bolt.
"Stand up, Aya."
She stares at me from her chair, eyes wide.
"Stand and take the Box you've been searching for all this time."
A short time passes.
But Aya does get to her feet.
She stands up, knowing what I'm going to do. Behind her, the light from the screen—*has created a small shadow.*
I look at her eyes. There is no doubt in them any longer.
She's prepared herself to receive it.
"Okay." First, I have to take her in. "Show me your crimes, Aya Otonashi!"

Then...
...I step on her shadow.

"——Ah."
I place my foot on the shadow, and I can see crimes.
The misdeeds of Aya Otonashi...no, of Maria Otonashi.
They...
They—

"——

        _____

            _____

                _____"

I've collapsed.
I lost consciousness.
Did I scream, I think? No, maybe I didn't.
I reflect on the memories I just witnessed.

These memories are not the most ugly or inhuman of all the thousand sins I've seen, but that doesn't have any bearing on the agony they bring. How they appear objectively doesn't matter; I receive the subjective suffering the person in question experienced when they committed their crimes.

That means Aya Otonashi hurt this badly back then.

It's like being stabbed through the heart by a thousand knives, like having my eyeballs crushed by a pair of pliers, like having my fingers pulled off one by one, like having a blender taken to my innards, like having long nails driven into each and every pore on my body. And it burns. This sin has aged and matured, turned into a thick liquid like molten iron that threatens to dissolve my body and reduce me to a formless mass.

What is this?

The shaking in my hands still won't stop. My pupils are fully dilated, and they won't return to normal.

She's—

She's been holding something like this the whole time?

"......Urgh!"

I wobble to my feet and give Aya Otonashi a long look.

I have to make Aya a Subject before I grant her the power as a Ruler. In order to do that, I have to choke down this shadow of a crime.

Aya will have to come face-to-face with this guilt once again. Can she remain unaffected when she's forced to confront it?

I have no intention of turning back, though.

There's no time for hesitation.

"Here goes."

I pull out Aya's shadow of a crime, the one I took into me when I stepped onto her shadow, and swallow it.

"——Nh!"

Aya's body goes taut, and she clutches her chest.

But that's all. I can't hide my amazement.

"......How are you still okay?"

Aya Otonashi is standing there impassively.

"I'm not okay."

At a closer glance, I can see a nervous sweat rising on her face. Her teeth are clenched, biting it back. But I even passed out for a moment because of this shadow of a crime; I can hardly believe her reaction is so mild.

"How are you standing? You shouldn't be able to take this. I know; I've experienced it firsthand."

"I presume this is meant to make me recall my own crimes?" she says.

Perspiration runs down her cheeks, yet Aya still manages to turn a forceful gaze in my direction.

"Yeah, and that's why you can't stand suddenly having to look right at it."

"It's not sudden."

"What?"

Aya releases her chest and takes a few deep breaths. You could pretty much say she's already back to normal.

"I feel this pain constantly. It's almost an old friend by now."

I don't grasp her meaning.

If I take her words at face value, though, that would imply...

What I did was to remind her of her crime. Of how she felt back then. Everyone else is able to live out their day-to-day by forgetting such pain, but what if that isn't the case for Aya? What if she's never let it leave her mind for even a second?

"I am always conscious of my crimes."

This hellish torment would be not an extraordinary experience, but a familiar one. If this pain is her constant companion, then she isn't going to lose herself just because I'm putting it in front of her.

"I'm beyond forgiveness. That's why—"

All the same, what the hell? Is that any way for a person to live?

No...I guess I get it.

So that's why.

"That's why—I can't live as a human."

It's the reason she was able to become "Aya Otonashi."

She thinks of herself as a sinner at all times. By never forgetting, she is continually punishing herself.

It's a just system of crime and punishment.

That's what made her into something that isn't human. Into a Box. Into "Aya Otonashi."

Having killed herself off entirely, she has enabled herself to make a wish with single-minded purpose. To stake everything, her whole way of life, on her mission.

For the sake of a world in which everyone can find happiness.

Her determination inspires many emotions in me.

Respect. Envy. Fascination. Unspeakable admiration.

She's the burned-out husk of an owner I will never become.

It's for this very reason that there's no worthier successor to my power.

Aya Otonashi.
Live on for the sake of wishes.

And you, Kazu.
I can't ever let you have "Maria Otonashi."
I will never allow you to crush our wishes.

"I'm going to give you my power. You're going to inherit all the shadows of crime."

Passing along the shadows of crime won't have any effect on me. It won't change my ability to Control my Subjects.

However, my most important task will be different.

My most important task is now to eliminate the power to do away with Boxes—Kazuki Hoshino, the boy with such deep influence on Aya Otonashi—and to help her persevere for the sake of our wishes.

"Are you ready?" I ask, but Aya doesn't look at me.

She's facing directly ahead.

"I pictured it," she nearly whispers. "I imagined what needed to be done to lead people to happiness, and what kind of Box I would need. It's not forcing people into a mold I've created. It's not helping them avoid the hardships of reality by dumping them in some hidden paradise, either. I came to believe that having each person give thought to the form of their own bliss and then move toward that is a fully realized happiness."

She clenches her fists tightly.

"That's why I needed the ability to guide others," she says, her voice rich with emotion. "To think I would find it here right in front me, after adjusting my viewpoint just a little."

Then she finally looks at me.

"Oomine. I had thought we were nothing more to each other than two people with their eyes set on the same course. But that isn't a small thing. That alone is enough for something like this to take place... I see—so this is what it means to be kindred spirits."

"Kindred spirits... You're right."

I nod, then transfer the shadows of crime.

This reminds me of a thought I had when I passed along shadows of crime to Shindo, that maybe someone strong enough could swallow down the shadows of other people's crimes as if it were nothing. And how if that were to happen, I would doubt my own adequacy as a Ruler.

"......Nnh."

Aya Otonashi receives 998 shadows of crime without batting an eye.

With that, she becomes a Ruler and, in keeping with my initial plan, my 999th Subject.

"Oomine," says the owner of Crime, Punishment, and the Shadow of Crime. "Thanks."

But her face is like a machine, without the slightest trace of happiness.

I make my way back to my own seat unsteadily, relying on the chairs to hold me up several times.

The lethargy presses down on me all at once like weights on my shoulders, and I can't move at all anymore.

All the same, I still have to think.

Now that Aya Otonashi is a Subject, there is one final obstacle to overcome in fulfilling my requirements for victory.

Summoning Kiri, the owner of the Silver Screen of Broken Wishes.

All I need to do is get her here, and then I can coerce Kazu into doing away with her Box.

"Kokone, I love you."

I react to the sound of my own voice coming from the speakers.

I've been watching the images on the screen for a bit now.

On it, I am embracing Kiri in a classroom. Tears stream from my eyes.

But even though my arms are around her, Kiri's hang limp and doll-like at her sides. She doesn't respond.

I say it again to help the words reach her.

"Kokone, I love you."

That's how she suffers.

Such directly expressed feelings bring her pain. Tears well up in her eyes.

What Kiri is feeling from me isn't unabashed love so much as a twisted obsession.

—*Don't abandon me. I love you too much.*

That's how she must hear it. It's a threat. A threat pressuring her not to change. A threat that asks her to remain the girl with no self-worth, who believes she is ugly and deserved those cigarette burns. That asks her to keep on suffering like this.

I was really an awful guy.

I couldn't be him any longer.

I had to change this world.

I had to correct the ones who had made her this way, who would try to do the same in the future. I wasn't cleaning the world of bad people. Rino and the others weren't bad people. No, they were just fools who lacked imagination. They can see only what's in front of them, not what lies beyond it. All I would be doing is righting that part of them. And if I could fix that, tragedies would no longer occur.

Kokone Kirino would be able to remain Kokone Kirino.

Right?

And all is as it should be.

Nothing else matters.

My happiness, Kiri's happiness—neither of them matter.

"—Yeah."

That's it. I've found it.

I need to use the Misbegotten Happiness on Kokone Kirino.

Someone whose spirit is already broken will want the Misbegotten Happiness. I'll use Kokone Kirino to erase Aya Otonashi's memory and make Kazuki Hoshino give up hope.

—Am I getting something wrong? I'm not, right?

The moment the idea of using Kiri arises, for some reason I also hit upon a means of getting her here.

It's easy, now that I think about it. As her childhood friend and former lover, I can conceive plenty of ways to lure her to me, obviously. If anything, how come it hadn't come to mind before now? Did I maybe have some sort of mental block?

I issue an Order to one of my fanatics. "Send an e-mail to the address I'm going to tell you now. The address is—"

I mentally write out Kiri's address from memory, then continue.

"Here's what it needs to say."

Kiri definitely won't come if I tell her to straight-out.

But I know she will if she thinks I'm crying for help. If she suspects I'm at the end of my rope, she's sure to come to my side. That's how she is. She's the type to place my happiness before her own.

I think of the message that would most effectively tell her I'm on the brink, then issue the Order to write it. It's the most despicable words I could say, and the most despicable line from the movie.

"Kokone, I love you."

All the same.

Yeah.

I *am* at the end of my rope.

◇◇◇ **Kazuki Hoshino 09/11 FRI 11:02 PM** ◇◇◇

"Maria became a Subject?"

I repeat Mogi's words without thinking.

"Kasumi...what does that mean? Wh-why would Maria...?" Haruaki asks Mogi, raising his head. He's still kneeling on the road.

"Th-that's just what Yanagi told me, so I don't really know any more..."

How could such a thing happen?

I was okay when Iroha stepped on my shadow, so Maria shouldn't have become a Subject when Daiya stepped on hers.

As long as she didn't want to.

"——!"

My phone suddenly rings with the sound of an incoming e-mail text. When I pull it out and start to open it, I hear another one.

"...Wh-what the?"

I can't help but feel uneasy about receiving two right in a row, now of all times.

On the screen is an unfamiliar e-mail address. The second one consists of only a single letter. *O*. More arrive even as I'm looking at it.

In total, there are eight texts from unknown senders, each arriving at five-second intervals, all containing just a single letter. In chronological order, they say:

F

o

r

g

e

t

m

e

Whether I like it or not, this tells me who the sender is.

"Maria...!"

Yes, it's true.

Maria has become a Subject.

No, it's probably something else, actually.

"Maria has given Orders to at least eight people..."

Maria has become a Ruler.

"...Why...has this happened...?"

During our confusion, yet another new text arrives. While the address of the sender is just as unfamiliar as before, this time, it contains more than a single letter.

Watch the news.

I swallow, then start up the 1seg app on my phone.

I find the program in question right away.

A female announcer is reading the details.

"This just in. Katsuya Tamura, one of the so-called dog-people with strangely doglike behavior, has come back to his senses. This is the first instance of recovery from this condition. According to the statement from the police force with Mr. Tamura in their custody, his mind is clear, and he is calm with no signs of confusion. Mr. Tamura has also stated that he has no memory of his time as a dog-person, and that he murdered his parents and is willing to make reparations for any crimes. ——We have a follow-up report. A suspect by the name of Yasumi Ishikawa, who had also become a dog-person, has come back to her senses......"

What's going on here? Why has Daiya returned his dog-people to normal now? Wasn't his plan to make people think about their ethical standpoint by mass-producing dog-people? Wouldn't reverting them undo all of that?

If so, then maybe Maria is the one responsible?

Assuming she is, why would Daiya allow it?

Right now, it almost looks as if it's Maria who holds the reins of Crime, Punishment, and the Shadow of Crime, doesn't it?

"......No way."

What if she actually does?

Could Maria have wanted to have Crime, Punishment, and the Shadow of Crime of her own free will? Could she have become a Subject, and then a Ruler, in order to use its abilities freely?

If she did, then why?

"—No, that..."

I understand everything.

If she did, I fully understand Maria's motives.

Her wish is to make other people happy—that's all. She wouldn't work toward any other purpose. So what she's doing here is meant to bring happiness to others.

In short, she's reached a decision.

A decision that Crime, Punishment, and the Shadow of Crime is a Box that can make others happy.

True, Maria had been seeking a Box. And the Box she obtained was Crime, Punishment, and the Shadow of Crime? The power to control other people?

"What the hell...?"

I clench my teeth.

Isn't that all but saying Daiya, not I, is the one who understands Maria and needs her?

I—

"I won't let her."

I know what Maria is going to do next now that she's taken Crime, Punishment, and the Shadow of Crime.

Unlike Daiya, Maria isn't going to do anything showy. She'll meet with each and every person the hard way, controlling them in the way that best suits them in an attempt to guide them to happiness.

It's an impossible, unending endeavor. It's spending her entire life in the service of others.

All the same, I'm sure Maria would be glad to devote the entirety of her time on earth to the joy of those around her.

She's happy to have made progress at long last.

"I won't let her." I say it again.

The only reason she thinks this is because she's under the sway of "Aya Otonashi."

She's acting to ignore her own happiness.

"...........I'll do it."

If so, then it's obvious how I'm going to respond.

"...........I'll crush it."

I won't let her have any hope as "Aya Otonashi."

I will plunge "Aya Otonashi" into despair.

"I'll crush Maria's Crime, Punishment, and the Shadow of Crime, too."

That hope you finally found? I don't give a damn.

Maria's cries and screams won't keep me from crushing that Box.

* ⋆ ⋆

My mind is made up.

The question is how.

Daiya can give Maria Orders. He can make as many demands of me as he wants. He could even threaten to Order Maria to use the Misbegotten Happiness on Yuri, if I make one false move.

Once he puts that out there, I'll have no choice but to comply with whatever it is he wants of me. If he tells me to destroy the Silver Screen of Broken Wishes, then I'll have to destroy it. If he tells me to watch Maria leave, then I'll have to watch her leave.

"—Grr."

So what's my best option?

Daiya is firmly blocking the path to Maria. If I don't find some means of fighting him, I'm going to lose before I can bring her back.

—*A way to fight him. A way to fight him...*

What I come up with is—

My gaze shifts over to Haruaki, who was asking me to do something a moment ago. He wanted me to take him and Kokone into the Silver Screen of Broken Wishes with me.

"Haruaki."

Yep, she really is the only way of fighting back against Daiya.

"Let's meet up with Kokone."

And then I shudder.

I'm considering something truly awful.

Mogi is kind enough to say she wants to help, but there's no way I'm taking her into the Silver Screen of Broken Wishes, so Haruaki and I head to meet Kokone after rushing her back to the hospital.

Since we had contacted her earlier, she's already waiting for us in the parking lot near the dorm where she's been hiding.

The instant we meet, Kokone hugs me with her head against my chest.

"Daiya said it," she tells me in a quavering voice. "He said he loves me."

She doesn't lift her face.

Even if she weren't shaking, I'd know she's crying.

"He's never said anything like that since I became this way."

Haruaki chews his lip wordlessly as he watches her.

"I've decided. No matter what anyone says." Kokone raises her face and turns her reddened eyes on me. "I'm going to save Daiya."

Her determination is immovable at this point.

"......Kokone."

That "I love you" probably came through some indirect message. It's a trap no matter how you slice it. But Kokone wouldn't listen even if I told her that.

Still, her resolve to see Daiya works out in my favor. It's perfect for the plan I have in mind.

"Will you do whatever it takes to help him?"

"I will. I'll risk anything. Even my life."

That's exactly the answer I want.

If I'm going to use Kokone as a countermeasure against Daiya, those are the words I need to hear.

"Let's go, Kokone, Haruaki. To the Silver Screen of Broken Wishes."

I'll even take advantage of Kokone's strong feelings for Daiya to get Maria back.

But Haruaki still smiles at me. "You're doing it! Thanks, Hosshi!"

He takes my hand with both of his. It's really firm.

"Th-that hurts, Haruaki."

Despite my protests, he doesn't loosen his hold.

There are tears pouring from his eyes as he gazes directly at me. "Thank you, Hosshi."

Still, there's no guarantee we'll be able to save Daiya just because Kokone is coming along.

Actually, Haruaki is crying only because this probably means he will be nearby when Daiya meets his end. He mistakenly believes I made my decision for Daiya's and Kokone's sakes.

Haruaki finally releases his grip on my hand.

My hand has gotten hot.

"Oh—"

My heart is quickly heating up, too, to an almost unbearable degree.

The two's sincere tears for Daiya are like an assault.

That's when I notice it.

"Unh...gh..."

I inspect my hand, burning after the heat of Haruaki's grip. This hand is the one that holds the power of crushing Boxes, of laying waste to wishes.

Possessing a hand like this makes me less human.

Taking advantage of their emotions, for Maria's sake, makes me less human.

After all, what I'm on the verge of doing is—

"AAAAaaaaah......"

When did I become so inhuman? Oh, maybe I was already crazy from the moment I tried to kill Iroha. I lost my way a long time ago, but it took me this long to realize because Iroha didn't happen to die.

I wish for happiness. I wish for the happiness of Daiya and Kokone and Haruaki. I want to cry alongside them. I want to help Daiya, with our hearts as one.

But I can't.

Maria will be mine again. This is my top priority, and nothing can change that. Nothing. That's who I am now.

I was remade to be this way when I obtained the Empty Box.

"Nn—nnnnnnnhhh......"

I start to cry.

But my tears aren't like Kokone's and Haruaki's, beautiful in their sympathy for another. They are selfish, shameful tears that only mean I regret my own nature.

"Haruaki, Kokone."

All I can do is be honest with them about my feelings.

"I love you two."

If nothing else, that is real. So unbelievably real.

Haruaki puts his arms around Kokone and me.

Kokone begins sobbing loudly.

I feel deeply guilty over how different my tears are from theirs. Kokone's tears wet my cheek. Sadness washes over me again as her innocence reminds me of how deeply sinful I am.

"I love you, but I may betray you."

The two of them look at me, their eyes round.

"I'm sorry. That won't stop me from doing whatever I have to for Maria's sake. I'll even make use of your feelings to take her back. Saving Daiya might be too much for me to do. I may even push him over the edge. And yet, I think—I really do think I want to help him. That's just a thought, though. I'm sorry. I'm sorry it's no more than a thought."

My tears don't stop.

"Please forgive me."

Neither of them speaks for a moment. We simply embrace one another in a circle.

The one who speaks up is Kokone. "You can't do anything about that." She continues in a tearful voice. "I'm only doing this to save Daiya, too. Haruaki wants me to be happy, but I'm sure he can't act on it."

Pushing against my chest, she breaks free from our circle of three and smiles.

"I'll forgive you, so you forgive me."

As I look at Kokone's and Haruaki's tears, something occurs to me.

Just like those four movies Daiya is watching, there isn't going to be a happy end to this tale, either.

Where did things go wrong?

When did the mistakes begin?

If everything was screwed up from the get-go, then was Daiya right in trying to fix the world?

I don't know.

I don't know, but we have to go.

To the shopping mall so that we can enter the Silver Screen of Broken Wishes.

To Daiya.

To Maria.

★   ★   ★

Before that, I'll mark myself to show I've strayed from the path of humanity.

Yeah, my right hand should do the trick. I'll carve my punishment into my right hand, the one with the power to crush Boxes.

And once that's done—

—let's go watch the credits of this story.

Theater 4

15 Years Old and Earrings

(3 / 3)

15 Years Old and Earrings, SCENE 4, 3/3

> *95. BACKGROUND - BLUE*
>
> KOKONE (VO)
> Please, I'm begging you.

> *96. BACKGROUND - WHITE*
>
> KOKONE (VO)
> Grant Daiya a happy future.

> *97. BACKGROUND - ALL BLACK*

> *98. BACKGROUND - ALL RED*

◆◆◆ Daiya Oomine 09/11 FRI 11:40 PM ◆◆◆

My thoughts are slipping away.

The imagery unfolding on the screen before me peels away at my very mind, taking me back in time. I fall into sync with the middle school me on-screen. My thoughts have become as they were back then. I can't tell where I am. Am I in my seat in the audience, on the screen, or in the past? The distinction doesn't mean much anymore.

My middle school self is cradling his head on the screen.

There are no lines spoken, but I know what my middle school self is saying over and over in his head. Now that I've gone back in time, I'm thinking the same thing.

—What could I have done?

—What could I have done?

—What could I have done?

But even though I'm about to break, I still haven't lost sight of what needs to be done. No matter how chaotic my mind is, I'm still holding a powerful sense of purpose that lets me act on autopilot.

Kazuki Hoshino is coming here.

I will take Kazu down and free Aya from his clutches.

And when I do, I will change the world.

Eventually, the door to the theater opens.

I turn my unfocused gaze to concentrate on a single point.

"Haven't seen you in a while."

Kazuki Hoshino is there.

Straining against the sluggishness of the Silver Screen of Broken Wishes, I get to my feet. It might have been difficult for me to stand even without the resistance at this point. I touch my earrings and turn around, trying to hide the strain even a little.

"Yeah. I feel that way, too," Kazu replies with a weak smile.

A plain plastic case is dangling from his hand. Did he make preparations or something before coming here? Now that he wields the ultimate weapon that is the power to crush Boxes, I can't see the point of anything extra. I decide not to worry about it.

That's why I'm even more interested in the state of his right hand and the weapon it holds than I am in the case.

"Kazu, what's up with your hand?"

It's wrapped in bandages. They're stained with blood, suggesting that the injury happened just recently.

"…This is my line in the sand."

That's all he says. Not a word more.

"He took a knife to his hand all of a sudden. A cut like that is gonna leave a scar for the rest of his life… I haven't got a clue why he did it, honestly…," Haruaki explains instead.

Instead of bothering to reply, I shift my gaze.

Over there is—Kokone Kirino.

—*Shunk*.

Seeing her is like a blade in my heart. I can't help it, but it's what I expected. Even having that fake, doll-like Kiri sitting next to me made a mess of my mind, so of course I'm going to react this way when I see the real thing.

My emotions don't matter, though.

"You're awfully bold showing up here. What do you plan to do, Kazu? You've gotta know you don't have a chance in hell. I've made Aya Otonashi my Subject."

I'm assuming Yanagi and Mogi leaked that part to him, too.

His expression unchanging, Kazu retorts, "Bold words from someone who looks so pale, Daiya."

The reply could be taken as a challenge, but Kazu is speaking with sympathy.

He takes a step forward.

Kazuki Hoshino and I are confronting each other.

Yeah—

Not a shred of doubt about it.

My face-off with Kazu began in the Game of Indolence, and now it ends here.

"Let's lay our plans out on the table, shall we?"

Kazu looks at me in silence.

"I will obliterate the Silver Screen of Broken Wishes. Then I will make Aya use the Misbegotten Happiness, doing away with her memories of you and leaving you broken." The first part of my approach is to destroy Kiri's Silver Screen of Broken Wishes with Kazu's Box-crushing power.

My next move will be to have the Misbegotten Happiness used on Kiri. "What do you have in store for me?"

"I'm going to destroy your Crime, Punishment, and the Shadow of Crime, whether by using my hand or by waiting out the twenty-four hours it takes for the Silver Screen of Broken Wishes to run its course. After that, I'll get rid of the Crime, Punishment, and the Shadow of Crime you gave to Maria, too."

Aya's eyebrows twitch when she hears that.

"Then I'll take Maria back."

Aya cuts in, her expression unchanged. "It'll be for nothing. I'm never going back to you, no matter what happens."

Kazu briefly worries his lip, but the light in his eyes as he glares at me remains the same.

"I—"

He bites down on those blood-soaked bandages.

"I won't turn back."

I notice something odd in his behavior that throws me off slightly. Undaunted, I'm about to open my mouth and put Kazu on the ropes—but then someone moves unexpectedly.

"Kazuki!" Yanagi rushes forward, toward Kazu, shouting as she leaps over the seats. "Destroy my Crime, Punishment, and the Shadow of Crime!"

Given how abruptly it happens, Kazu is almost frighteningly unperturbed. He holds out his bandaged hand to Yanagi's chest as she runs up to him.

And then it plunges into her.

"Nn...ah...ahhh!"

Yanagi gasps, impaled on his arm.

Kazu pulls a black Box out of her chest, small enough to fit comfortably in his hand. It's shaped like a piece of *konpeito* candy, all spiny and painful-looking to hold.

Not even glancing at the Box, Kazu obliterates it without a second thought.

"Ahhh..."

Yanagi loses consciousness and collapses on the spot.

Kazu's eyes shift down to look at her on the ground.

The series of actions is so smooth, it's as if he's a programmed machine.

A momentary hush falls.

Eventually, I realize Yanagi's intent. She had her Crime, Punishment, and the Shadow of Crime neutralized as quickly as possible, thinking I might try to exploit her with an Order. She moved so quickly to give Kazu the slightest bit of an advantage.

There's no way I could have foreseen her actions; I didn't think Yanagi knew he had the ability to destroy Boxes. She must have listened in on my conversation with O and kept that knowledge hidden until this very moment.

While she did manage to pull one over on me, I never had any intention of using her to begin with. This doesn't affect my plan at all.

Still, I've broken out in a mild sweat.

I did just witness it, after all.

"The power to crush Boxes..."

Yes, his overwhelming ability that breaks all the rules.

Actually seeing it feels so different from just hearing about it. It's like having a machine gun pointed in my face and someone's finger on the trigger.

One misstep, and Crime, Punishment, and the Shadow of Crime is history.

And then there's his complete lack of hesitation. His expression didn't change when his power was put to use.

I'm reminded of something. Kazu isn't the same person he was back when we were on friendly terms. This Kazu does crazy things like scarring his own right hand; he's been completely reborn.

As a being meant to destroy Boxes.

As a being meant to oppose O.

And that's why his smile can be so similar to O's.

That expression didn't change even when he destroyed the Box, but it twitches when someone else speaks.

"What is that power?" Aya asks, and his face goes stiff. "Kazuki Hoshino. Why do you have this ability? ...No, that doesn't matter. Now that I've seen what you can do, I'm certain."

It seems painful for her to say it.

"You are my enemy."

Kazu bites down on his lip.

Of course, hostility from the one he's trying to win back, the one he wants to save more than anyone else, is going to sting.

"Aya, I'm sure you know this, but keep your distance from Kazu. I'm sure he'll crush your Crime, Punishment, and the Shadow of Crime without batting an eye."

"...Good call. That ability lets him destroy Boxes with just a touch to the chest. Even the Misbegotten Happiness is in danger."

"No, he won't do away with the Misbegotten Happiness. I think he knows that would result in the fracturing of your entire personality from the foundations up."

A look at Kazu's expression confirms I'm correct.

"Naturally, I'm not going anywhere near him, either."

Now that we've reached this point, I must act with complete precision.

"So here are my demands. Destroy Kiri's Silver Screen of Broken Wishes."

"Daiya..." Kokone calls my name.

Before that voice can stir up any emotion within me, I push on with instructions for Kazu.

"You know what happens if you don't do what I tell you, right? Let me remind you: Aya Otonashi is a Subject. I can make her do whatever I want. I'm not letting you try anything funny, either, Kazu. Okay, let's set a time limit. It's forty minutes past the hour, right? Destroy Kiri's Silver Screen of Broken Wishes by eleven forty-five."

"......"

Kazu goes quiet.

He can try to search for, or perhaps create, an opening in my defenses to smash Crime, Punishment, and the Shadow of Crime.

I know he brought Haruaki and Kokone here to help him find such an opportunity.

Kazu will do everything he can to strike at a chink in my armor, while I won't let him find a single tiny one. This is the kind of battle we're fighting.

Now, time for Kazu's offensive to begin.

"Daiyan, just give it up already. I can't stand to see this."

As I suspected, his attack kicks off with Haruaki's attempts to reason with me.

"What's the point? Who is this helping? Not you. Not Kiri. You'd know that if you could see yourself now, right? At this rate, nobody's going to be happy. This is just going to end badly for both of you."

Still, just because I expected it and mentally prepared myself doesn't mean he didn't get to me. Haruaki is so honest and straightforward.

"Please. Stop this, for Kiri's sake, too."

I don't make any response.

"Please... Please..."

Haruaki is crying now. This entreaty is from the heart.

I start thinking to myself.

Haruaki is like a brilliantly shining light; he is and always has been. I've got nothing on him.

He's the first person in my life who I've ever felt has me beat, and not just in his talent for baseball. It's his candor. His lack of hypocrisy. His steadfast determination to do what he thinks is right that allowed him to throw away his inherent gift for baseball and feelings for the girl he loves. Haruaki has a charisma I could never have no matter how much I may want it.

That's why the idea of making him into a Subject never entered my mind.

You know, Haruaki? I respect you more than you can imagine.

"Quit sitting there all quiet and answer me, Daiyan!"

Regardless.

I'm not going to give up on this wish.

"Okay, then who's going to do it if not me?" I have no doubts. "Whose fault is it that Kiri ended up this way? Mine? Kiri's? Rino's? Yeah, it's probably on all of us. That's not what this is about, though. That isn't the underlying problem. Which is why I'm going to make changes at the roots. That's what I'm saying."

Haruaki appears to struggle a little finding the words, but he retorts, "That's reckless. There's no way you can pull it off, even with a Box."

"It's not a matter of whether I can or can't. I am doing it."

"But why does it need to be you? You're already in pain; why should you have to suffer more?"

"I've decided to sacrifice myself."

"What about how I feel?! I don't want to see you and Kiri on this crash course! Are you ready to sacrifice my feelings, too?!"

I answer immediately. "Yes."

Haruaki's eyes go wide.

"That's what it means to sacrifice myself."

Haruaki is rendered speechless.

Yes, that's what it means to sacrifice myself. I understand this full well.

I will sacrifice the feelings of those who care for me, too.

That's why I cut them off. Both Kiri and Haruaki.

"Don't be stupid..." He's shaking, his fists clenched. "Don't be stupid... Daiyan..."

It would seem Haruaki's offensive is at an end. I look away from him and back to Kazu, with more hostility.

"Kazu, get on with it. Hurry up and crush the Silver Screen of Broken Wishes."

I casually wipe away the thick sweat covering my forehead. I'm playing it cool, and inside, I'm calm, but I'm taking damage here.

After Haruaki's forthright emotions, the shadows of crime are on the verge of running wild. I can't take much more. The shadows of crime could split my body open and come gushing out at any moment.

My mind is done for. A word might make me want to just end it all, though I don't know what it would be.

Will abandoning everything release me?

But I—

I look at Aya Otonashi.

But I—I will die embracing all these crimes.

I press down hard on my hammering chest.

All right, I need to get ready.

I'm awaiting the next assault. One screwup, and I'll be down for the count.

Next is a surefire attack.

★   ★   ★

"Daiya, thank you for the message."

Kokone Kirino.

Kiri is walking toward me.

Still pressing my chest, I say with some effort, "It was a trap to lure you here. Looks like you took the bait."

"Oh, I knew it was a trap."

"I'm sure you did."

Kiri is still coming closer.

The one who cares for me more than anyone else is still coming my way.

One step at a time, Kokone Kirino draws near.

The expression may seem a little trite, but with every step, the distance between us shrinks, and memories of our past flash before my eyes, like the beam of a lighthouse.

Age four—I make her cry when the two of us are squabbling over some candy at preschool, so the teacher scolds me. I cry, too.

Age seven—I help Kiri grab on to a life preserver when she almost drowns at the beach, then try to calm her down as I bring her to shore.

Age nine—After Kiri and I get separated at a festival, I find her in her *yukata*, sitting by the side of the road in tears, and I lead her home by the hand.

Age eleven—Our classmates have started giving me the cold shoulder because of our relationship. Upset, I tell Kiri I hate her and other awful things, making her cry. I go to her house and apologize.

Age twelve—Kiri stays home from school when I tell her I got accepted to an elite private middle school. The next time she comes to school, I tell her I'm not going to enroll. She, of course, starts bawling.

Age fourteen—Our first kiss. She starts crying afterward. Unsure of what to do, I just keep rubbing her head until the tears stop.

For some reason, Kiri is crying in all my memories. It's probably because the most powerful image I have of her is her leaning on me.

Yeah, but this is still hard on me.

Every one of those memories is a blow, an attempt to keep me locked into normality. Every one is like a heavy mass hanging around my shoulders.

As she tortures me with my own past, Kokone Kirino reaches me. The husk of her created by the Silver Screen of Broken Wishes is there, too.

One Kiri's face is right above the other's.

Standing in front of me, she lifts her chin slightly and gazes into my eyes.

"Daiya, about that message you sent me—this is my reply."

And then—

"I love you, too."

—*she embraces me.*

"Wha...?!"

This shouldn't be possible.

It shouldn't be possible for her to take me in her arms anymore.

Whenever she does, she remembers everything that happened, the pain of her back, and throws up.

And yet, here she is with her arms around me now.

Don't tell me she's overcome the horrors of what she's experienced?

But she tells me, "Hey, Daiya. I still can't get over it. I'm still as broken as ever, and I don't know what to do."

Then—why you are able to put your arms around me?

"But there is something I do know."

Kiri tells me.

"You're all I have."

Kiri is trembling. As she says, it's not that she's moved on. She's simply fighting back the feelings tormenting her so she can embrace me.

That's all she can do.

"I love you. I love you... I love you."

Yeah, I can't help but think, *the two of us really do hurt each other when we're together.*

And yet, what if we could triumph over everything if we both felt the same way?

It goes without saying, but...that's something I had wanted to believe all along.

"Urgh."

I remember something else.

The day when I tried to change the world.

"It's cold."

Kiri rejected me in that cold red water lit by the setting sun. Unable to embrace her, all I could do was feel the growing chill in my body and hers. I was utterly powerless.

Still, if we can embrace as we are now...

If I can still bring warmth to Kiri's body now, even when I was so cold back then...

"Ungh—"

Kokone.

Hey, I want to rest, too.

If I'm really all you need, it would be so easy. I'd do anything for you, Kokone. It wouldn't hurt at all.

"I would do anything for you, Daiya."

Those words snap me back to my senses.

I push against Kiri's shoulders with my arms to separate myself from her embrace.

"Daiya?"

Kiri would do anything for me?

I would do anything for her?

We would.

That's why it's wrong.

It's not healthy. Not normal. It's aberrant.

It wasn't like that. We used to be a much more average couple. A pair of typical lovers—we wouldn't think of throwing away our own lives and acting only for each other's sake.

We've changed to become that way, and that's the greatest proof that we can't make it in the normal world. We tear each other apart with our mutual self-sacrifice, and that's the reality. This is even truer if Kiri says I'm all she has.

Yeah, there really is no going back for us.

No going back to those days of innocence.

Do you have a wish?

I do.

I have one, all right.

I want to annihilate the world that transformed all our memories into pain.

I swore it on that day, in that red, red water.

"I will change the world."

I won't cast aside that part of me. I won't remove the earrings I've put in.

And that's why I abandon these sentiments, these memories, these recollections.

"You..." Harshly, I tell Kiri, "You need to be able to live in a world without me."

That is my answer.

Tears stream from Kiri's wide eyes.

I look away from her and toward Kazu instead.

Sure enough, I weathered that attack, too. Kazu can't have anything more potent lined up.

I look at my watch. It's forty-four minutes after the hour.

"Time's up. Crush Kiri's Silver Screen of Broken Wishes now. You know what's going to happen to Aya Otonashi if you don't, right?"

"It's too bad," Kazu replies softly. "I wished it wouldn't come to this."

Kazu begins crying again and falls to his knees.

"Nh... Nh..."

Kiri moves away, realizing there is no more getting through to me, and totters over toward a spot directly beneath the center of the screen.

Kazu gets to his feet and moves in that direction, too.

My line of sight naturally follows them toward the screen.

"I would give my all for your happiness."

The Kiri on the screen says her lines with empty eyes.

"If I ever stand in the way, I'll make it easy to get rid of me."

⋆　　⋆　　⋆

"Daiya."

Kiri says my name. She's standing in front of the center of the screen, cutting off the light from the projector.

"You expect this to destroy you, right?"

"Yeah, that's the plan," I reply matter-of-factly.

"Do you think I'd let that happen?"

"And why would I need your permission to—?"

"I won't let you do it."

Then Kiri—

—stabs herself in the stomach with the knife she'd hidden on her.

Blood spatters across the screen.

A dumbfounded "Wha—?" escapes my mouth before I can think.

I'm left in a pathetic state of uncomprehending shock. All I can do is watch the bloodstains spread on the screen.

It's Kazu who springs to action and runs to Kiri's side.

I take it for granted that he intends to help her.

But he doesn't.

"I really hate that I have to resort to this, Daiya."

Kazu plants himself in front of Kiri as if to prevent me from reaching her.

"I did what you said. *The Silver Screen of Broken Wishes will still be destroyed this way, right?"*

Instead of helping her, he steps in the blood pouring out of her.

"What…are you saying?"

"All right, Daiya." Kazu ignores my question and glares at me, angrily wiping away his tears. *"If you come anywhere near Kiri, I'll crush your Crime, Punishment, and the Shadow of Crime."*

He then sets down the plastic case in his hand.

"This is a first aid kit. Kokone won't die right away with where she stabbed herself, but she will for sure if nothing is done in ten minutes or so. On the other hand, if I stop the bleeding and give her first aid, there's a good chance she'll pull through. I told her to stab herself there. Kokone will die if you just wait there like an idiot, though. She'll probably be gone by the time midnight rolls around, and so will the Silver Screen of Broken Wishes. You'll get your way out with Crime, Punishment, and the Shadow of Crime still in hand. Once you escape, you can use the Misbegotten Happiness on whoever's around and get rid of Maria's memory, too. *But Kokone will die.*"

Beneath that screen drenched in blood, Kazuki Hoshino makes his demand.

"*If you want to help Kokone, then get over here and let me crush Crime, Punishment, and the Shadow of Crime.*"

He may not realize it himself.

But it's right there on Kazuki Hoshino's face.

Right there on the face of the Box destroyer.

An enchanting smile, just like O's.

"To be honest, I have my doubts."

Kazu's tone is dispassionate.

"You said you chose to abandon Kokone and change the world, but do you really mean it?"

He looks at the blood soaked into his bandages as he speaks.

"*I want you to show that you actually do.*"

"_____"

I'm speechless.

I can parse what Kazu is saying. But I don't get his line of thinking. None of the pieces fit.

I've misjudged him.

Kazu's bizarre nature is something I've always known. I had even observed that his abnormality is getting worse.

I never expected it had come this far, though.

Yeah, it's just as Aya said. As long as his objective is intact, he has no concept of giving up. He'll take measures to achieve it that no normal person would ever consider.

He's even capable of doing away with his own will once his target is in sight. It's almost as if he's acting on autopilot.

That, in a certain sense, is how I should strive to be. It's an ideal character trait for making my wish come true.

Still—

Seeing Kazu's smile makes me think.

—I may want to become Aya Otonashi, but I don't want to become this.

Nobody says a word. The only sounds come from the audio of the movie playing on indifferently, and Kokone's moans.

It's Haruaki who breaks the silence.

"Hosshi, you...didn't tell me about this! I had no idea this is how you were going to do it!"

"Sorry, but I had to keep you in the dark. I knew you would try to stop me otherwise."

"Of course I would! You're...insane! Even if Daiya doesn't step up, you know *I'm* going to help Kiri!"

"If you try anything, I'll finish her off."

"What?!"

"I mean it, okay?"

I'm sure he does mean it. If he can follow through with a plan this thoroughly twisted already, then he really must. Cutting his own hand was crazy enough; he wasn't lying when he called it "a line in the sand."

Haruaki seems to have caught on to that as well, because he doesn't say anything more. He just stares, his shoulders trembling.

A question slips out of my mouth.

"Kazu, are you going to be okay with it if Kokone dies like this?"

"What a weird question," Kazu replies. "Obviously not."

The answer is remarkably similar to a certain girl's, one who spent a lifetime becoming someone else.

"I'll regret it for the rest of my life. The guilt will constantly weigh on my mind, maybe enough to break me."

There's something different about it, though.

"I know that, but I'm still doing it."

Unlike Aya, Kazu isn't even making a choice.

Maybe—*he doesn't have one.*

The actions he's taking might confuse him, too, but he can't do anything else. That's the nature of his madness.

"Kazuki Hoshino...," mutters Aya. "You have lost your mind!" She bites down on her lip for a moment, then launches into a rant. "This isn't even a means to an end. An idea like this would never occur to an ordinary person. This... This is taking advantage of Kirino because you know she can't keep her head straight when it comes to Oomine. You go through with this, and that normal life you supposedly love will be shattered once and for all. You knew that before, right? 'Insane' is the only word for it."

She's exactly right.

"You really aren't the Kazuki Hoshino I know anymore. What the hell have you become? A hungry spirit? A demon?"

Kazu seems saddened, but he answers without missing a beat. "I'm a knight."

"A knight?"

"I will rescue Maria, even if it means fighting all of humanity. To that end, I will defeat, slay, and make corpses of anyone who would stand in my way."

"I never asked for that! Especially not from a fiend like you!"

"Nothing you say will deter me." Still sorrowful, Kazu says, "My only course leads to you."

Stunned, Aya falls silent.

Kazu looks away from her and speaks to me. "By the way, Daiya—aren't you going to help Kokone?" he asks so easily.

"I can't make up my mind."

His reply is unbelievable.

"Okay, then forget about it."

"Huh?" I can't hide my shock at his reaction. "Forget about it? You've gotta be kidding. You're saying you're okay with letting Kokone die because I can't make up my mind? You just want me to decide to save Kokone, right?"

"Daiya. You of all people should know who I'm doing all this for," Kazu retorts, brushing aside my question.

I, of course, know the answer. First, last, and always, he is working for Aya.

"Maria has Crime, Punishment, and the Shadow of Crime, right? She's going to try to use it to save the world, or at least make it a little better. Right?"

Kazu opens and closes his bandaged right hand in front of his face. It's as if he's making certain of something.

"Nobody needs a Box that does that. Which is why I'll crush it."

That's when I finally understand.

"—Don't tell me," I whisper.

The corners of Kazu's mouth twitch. "So you've put two and two together. I told you earlier that I had my doubts. When it comes to Maria, though, I'm certain. I spent an entire life's worth of time with her. I'd never get it wrong."

Aya Otonashi lives for the happiness of others.

Which means she can't let others give their lives for her.

And there's someone bleeding out right in front of her now.

If so—

"Aya will go help her even if I don't."

Yeah, I had thought this trap was meant for me.

But not exactly.

It's both a trap for me and one for Aya.

"Yeah." I can hear her pain. "I'll help Kirino. I'll have to go near Kazuki Hoshino and his power."

"Aya…! Isn't this the Box you've been searching for all this time?!"

"It is. It's the Box I spent an entire lifetime trying to find. It could have given me everything I wanted. I may never get this opportunity again. I know… I know—but."

Aya clenches her fists.

"But I still have to."

Yeah. That's the way "Aya Otonashi" is.

Kazuki Hoshino is fighting so dirty, he'd even use her nature against us.

In a moment, Aya will go in front of the screen to save Kiri, and Kazu will annihilate Crime, Punishment, and the Shadow of Crime. Kiri will survive thanks to Aya's first aid. The screening of *15 Years Old and Earrings* will end, and then the final stage of the Silver Screen of Broken Wishes will run its course. And thus, my Crime, Punishment, and the Shadow of Crime will be destroyed.

All our wishes will be completely finished.

There's a way to stop this.

Aya is my Subject. I could Order her not to move.

But...

But that would be...

"Daiya." Kazu says what I'm thinking aloud. "Don't tell me you'd stoop to using an Order to leave Kokone to her fate?"

Yes. He's right.

I thought I had decided to put a stop to this, no matter what it takes.

I thought my heart was sure all this time.

If so—then will I go to such lengths as using an Order to stop Aya and let Kiri die? Will I end her life myself?

What the hell?

What the hell?

What the goddamn *hell*?!

"A...agh."

Blood trickles from Kiri's mouth.

She tilts her head, turning her face my way.

Weakly, she whispers:

"Please, I'm begging you.

"I don't care if I die, so...

"...grant Daiya a happy future."

She starts to cry.

It's exactly like in all those memories of her depending on me.

"Kokone."

All of them.

All the movies of the Silver Screen of Broken Wishes play through my head once more in a flash.

Kokone Kirino. Haruaki Usui. Aya Otonashi. Miyuki Karino. Koudai Kamiuchi. Each and every one of them a tragedy, meant to make me suffer. The images line up like a series of file folders, binding my body and burning themselves in my mind one by one. The denial, the denial, the denial—I can't accept it. Nothing is ever kind. My vision goes black and white, then color, then sepia, then black and white again. The emotions in these images force their way into me, painting me over. I'm pushed out of my own body, and all that's left is Kokone Kirino. *I wanted to destroy the world, but I was thinking only of you. Only of you. Only of you.*

Yes, that's how the shadows of crime devour me. Consume me. Swallow me down. The pack of wild beasts has caught me at last and begins to devour all of who I am. There is no pain. Black blood wells up from beneath the fangs piercing my body and covers the world. My form vanishes as every last bit of it is eaten. I am a swamp of black blood. The swamp cannot think.

The swamp ruminates on a memory.

The sunset has taken over this cold red world. In the middle of the cold red light is a girl standing there all by herself. She enters the cold red water, her back turned the entire time. It makes a sound. I want her to turn back turn back turn back turn back turn back. I reach out—and take the girl's hand.

Then I tell her:

"—I *will change the world. I will change the world for you.*"

Time is running out. Not until the Silver Screen of Broken Wishes reaches its end—but until Kokone dies.

Time is running out.

"——Yeah."

I had intended to change the world. I had intended to create swarms of dog-people, making everyone keenly aware of right and wrong and thus enhancing their moral perspective. I had intended to do away with anyone who shut their mind off. I didn't care if I rotted away as long as there was someone to take up my cause after me. I had believed Iroha Shindo might be up to the task. I had been certain Aya Otonashi could do it. I would create a kind world free of tragedy where anyone could stand firm with confidence. I would create a world where the things that happened to us would never happen again. I was willing to make the sacrifices needed. I would even give up my own soul.

A kind world.

A just world.

Yes, I long for it, deeply. More, more, more than anyone. There's nothing false about my earnest wish.

But... ·

...despite that...

...the pool of blood before my eyes is just too much.

——I know.

I've always known.

Yes,

The truth is,

When I grabbed your hand

In that red world,

All I needed

Was for you

To turn back.

Where am I?

It's a red movie theater. Right, a theater.

That's why a movie is playing.

My actions and the images in front of me are in perfect sync.

"I..."

"I..."

I fall to my knees.

So does the boy in middle school.

"I couldn't care less what happens to me."

"I couldn't care less what happens to me."

I cover my tears with both hands.

So does the boy in middle school.

"All I've ever wanted is for you to be happy."

"All I've ever wanted is for you to be happy."

★ ★ ★

"Kokone."
And thus, I—
"I'll save you."

—am defeated.

My eyes open.
They were never closed, but now they are truly open.
Aya is reaching for the first aid kit.
Without a moment's delay, Kazu reaches for her chest and removes the Box. The Crime, Punishment, and the Shadow of Crime I gave to her.
Hers is a clean cube-shaped Box.
And Kazu obliterates it.
Though her Box is destroyed, Aya stays conscious and continues tending to Kokone.

I can't do anything anymore.
I can't move. I can't even resist the lethargy of the Silver Screen of Broken Wishes anymore.
So I just watch the last moments of *15 Years Old and Earrings*.
The final scene is in a hallway at a middle school.
Looking at my right ear, Kokone asks me sadly, *"You…got an earring?"*
Now with silver hair, I answer. *"Yeah, because I hate earrings."*
"Is that…" Kokone continues, her expression still sorrowful. *"…your way of asking for help?"*

Someone's alarm goes off.
"It's midnight," Haruaki says quietly.

In the same instant, the abyss, the pitch-black hole that's finally made its way to me, attacks. The abyss penetrates my chest, gnaws into me, and forces its way into my body. The theater converges into the abyss, shrinking into a round shape.

As absolute nothingness overtakes me, I feel something.

Loss.

And then I know.

My Crime, Punishment, and the Shadow of Crime is gone.

The movie theater begins to lose its form until it is nothing more than a red orb. The abyss grows equally massive in inverse proportion, absorbing me more and more.

Once I'm completely drawn into the abyss, what spreads through me is not darkness, but light.

Light.

And as the light fills every corner of me, someone taps me on the shoulder.

◇◇◇ Kazuki Hoshino 09/12 SAT 12:00 AM ◇◇◇

We're in front of the cinema complex on the third floor of the shopping mall. We've been transported here with our relative positions from within the Silver Screen of Broken Wishes intact.

An ambulance wails nearby. We had contacted them earlier, so it should be here soon. The spot where I instructed Kokone to stab herself is less lethal than I told Daiya. At the very least, she won't be dying in ten minutes. There's also the fact that Maria is applying first aid, and she has medical knowledge. Unless we're extremely unlucky, Kokone will make it. If she recovers without any major complications, then everything will have gone as I planned. Still, even if the plan goes off without a hitch—

I'm sorry, Kokone. I'm truly sorry.

I gaze into the distance, not looking at her where she lies. The mall is empty. There really is something unnerving about this aspect of the place, since you normally never see it. I remember the four of us, including Maria, shopping here at some point. She did dress me up like a girl, but it was a fun page of my normal life. But my memories of this building are tainted with blood, and that won't ever change.

That is how my normal life crumbles away.

I lower my gaze. There are *six people* here. Me. Haruaki, clenching his fists. Kokone, collapsed and bleeding. Maria treating her. And then—

Daiya looks at the owner of the hand on his shoulder, his eyes wide.

"That's right, Daiya," I tell him. "You had it wrong. You were going to lose from the very beginning."

I glance at my accomplice's face and then continue.

"Yes, the owner of the Silver Screen of Broken Wishes...is Miyuki Karino."

Miyuki Karino.

In her high school uniform, she gazes sadly into Daiya's face.

Everything started when I learned she had obtained a new Box. Just as owners can sense the Boxes of others, I gained the ability to sense them once I started coming under a Box's powerful influence.

Hers was devoted entirely to Daiya Oomine. Knowing this, I gave up on becoming an owner myself and decided to use her.

"You would have been able to see her, if only you could have faced yourself. You even would have realized she's the owner. But you couldn't see any of it."

Daiya stares at me in silence.

"Because you were avoiding confronting her."

Karino wordlessly moves away from Daiya.

Even though she went to such lengths and created this Box, she has nothing to say to him.

"Karino's wish was to have you all to herself. But the Box would grant that wish along with her negative feelings. While she does love you, she still holds on to a hatred for you and how you still bring her pain. She also knows it's impossible for you to be hers alone."

That's why the Silver Screen of Broken Wishes tortured Daiya by showing him the past. Why it tried to rob him of his precious wish. And...why it was effective for only a single day.

"It's not me, and it's not Kokone. Karino is the only one who could possess such a distorted Box. You would have known that, if only your eyes were open to it. But this is what it came to."

Positive that the owner was Kokone Kirino, Daiya hadn't considered anyone else.

Because he needed to blind himself in order to work toward his wish.

"Since I knew the truth, I could tell that your inability to see yourself was why you asked me so much about my conviction and my resolve. But you still kept walking toward your own downfall, so for me, it always......"

My voice suddenly quavers here.

The emotions I had kept bottled up during my face-off with Daiya come pouring out.

I look at Kokone all covered in blood.

Why did I ever do this?

My normal life will likely never return. I've hurt Kokone so much. I put this plan into action without telling Haruaki, and that rift between us won't just disappear. My friendship with him will never go back to what it once was.

How did I get here?

I had no choice but to do what I did, though.

Now that I have the Empty Box.

"For me, it always..."

The emotions well up, and tears stream from my eyes.

"...just looked like you were crying out."

That's right—in the end...

...I had no choice but to take down a friend who was screaming in pain.

"Enough," Daiya mutters, his head still lowered. "Enough about all that."

He limps slowly over to the bloodstained girl on the ground.

"*Kokone.*"

She's breathing painfully as he looks down at her and calls her name.

Daiya touches one of the earrings in his right ear. It's the first earring he ever got.

He rips it out.

Blood drips from his ear, but Daiya just grips Kokone's hand with an expression so gentle, it's as if he doesn't even feel the pain.

"Kokone."

He says her name again, then adds:

"I love you."

His expression is a smile from some other time, the kind of smile no one ever would have seen outside of those movies.

Epilogue

The school day is once again going to end before I exchange a single word with anyone, it seems.

Lunch break. I stretch and look out the window. The weather is fine, and the gentle sunlight is pouring into the classroom. I hear there's a typhoon coming tomorrow, though.

An unexpected pain runs across the back of my right hand. The wound has closed, but it still twinges when I remember it.

When I remove the bandages, the scar still runs straight along my hand. Each time I see it, I think:

The things I've done won't go away.

I faintly sigh as I scan all the empty seats in the classroom.

Kokone is still in the hospital. Her life isn't in danger, but that doesn't mean her injury is insignificant. What's worse, she's now going to have a scar on her abdomen, too, as well as the symbol on her back.

Mogi is still in the hospital as before. Though she doesn't appear any different on the surface, I get the feeling she's a little more distant with me.

As for Yuri, her involvement in this put a burden on her that might have been too much. She's been staying home from school a lot recently, including today. Though she does appear to enjoy speaking with me, it hurts me to see how obviously down she is.

Iroha refuses to see me. According to Yuri, she claims she's fine and there's no need to worry about her, but it's possible she's saying that just to put me at ease.

I haven't spoken with Haruaki once since it ended.

I leave the classroom.

I suddenly don't feel like going to my afternoon classes. Spending time in this empty classroom is just agonizing any way I think about it.

I head to the shoe cupboard. In the hallway, I pass by a few girls and overhear them mention "dog-people" in their conversation.

Dog-people.

In the end, the dog-people never became a worldwide phenomenon. All the former dog-people recovered their memories at once, which led society to accept that the situation had been mostly resolved. Without the mystique, the incident fell out of the news cycle, and the talk shows that had once featured the dog-people day after day quickly found new fodder from the affair between a mainstream idol group and an entrepreneur.

That's how powerful of an incident it was. I'm sure most people haven't completely forgotten about the dog-people. But the topic now feels distinctly in the past.

The dog-people have run their course as a subject of conversation.

That's how things are now. At the very least, the dog-people didn't prompt anyone to deeply ponder their morality. Pretty much no one talks about them online anymore. The Internet is flooded with all kinds of news every day. Right now, the biggest talking point is a manga writer who said some nasty things to a fan. This led to more people yelling at one another, and now it's a full-blown shitstorm. Someone even got arrested for sending a death threat to the author. It makes me cringe a bit to think that this is on the same level as what Daiya caused.

All that said, I don't think Daiya's actions were meaningless. There are probably people out there who are still thinking about the issues he brought up. But he would have needed to keep it up if he wanted to hold the attention of society. The fact is that news has an expiration date.

I arrive at the shoe cupboard. No one reprimands me or stops me as I switch from my indoor shoes to my leather ones.

In the schoolyard, I spot people playing basketball and catch.

Even in a school as full of Subjects as this one, daily life rolls on with little or no change. The Subjects have all lost their memories of the Box. I'm sure there are some individuals among them who were greatly affected. But even that doesn't appear to have had any influence on the normal day-to-day of school.

"......"

Why is that?

Seeing it puts me in a little bit of a bad mood. Even though I stopped Daiya's plans, even though this is exactly what I wanted, the fact that nothing has changed doesn't really make me happy.

I mean, if that's the case, then what are any of us even capable of?

If Daiya can step forward alone with the resolve to let his goals destroy him, and still nothing changes, what does that say about the rest of us? What does it say about our daily lives that they go on just the same regardless of whether one of us is seriously injured or leaves school or just vanishes?

...No, that viewpoint is too similar to Daiya's.

If anything, that's exactly why I have faith in normality. I have faith that, if normal life is able to correct so many extreme changes, I can save Maria by pulling her into it.

The reason I'm getting all sentimental is because I am Daiya's friend, even though he might say otherwise now. I just want him to get *something* for his efforts.

"Daiya..."

Daiya has disappeared again.

I met with him only once after everything, when he came to school after he had officially withdrawn. His hair was black, and he had removed his earrings. I mustered up the courage to speak with him, but all he did was give me a little smile without actually having a conversation.

I have no idea what he intends to do from here on out.

Leaving school, I ride the train and arrive at the five-story apartment building I'm so used to visiting. I've never pressed any buttons in this elevator except for the ones for the first and fourth floors, and I probably won't have a reason to press any others. As always, I punch the button for the fourth floor and head to the door of room 403.

Inserting my copy of the key, I open the door.

Before me is a completely bare room.

No one is here.

Kicking off my shoes, I make myself at home in this empty apartment once again. There's no trace of Maria's presence anywhere, though.

Anywhere.

I could handle the lack of furniture or decorations. There wasn't much of anything in here to begin with, after all.

But there's one little thing that's more than I can stand—it doesn't smell like peppermint.

It was basically Maria's scent to me, and now it's gone.

That makes reality sink in that, whether I like it or not, Maria will not be returning to this apartment.

"Maria…"

She's gone.

After she finished treating Kokone that day, Maria vanished. I don't recall turning my attention away from her, which means Maria had most likely been waiting for a chance to slip away from me. I went searching right away, but I could find neither hide nor hair of her.

Though she is apparently still enrolled in school, I don't think she'll be coming back. That's why she cleared out the apartment.

She probably doesn't plan on seeing me ever again.

Sure, I intend to take Maria back. Of course. I should be able to.

But—I can't.

Just finding Maria gone ends my search before it begins.

"——Ah, ahhh!"

I'm having trouble breathing. It feels as if all the oxygen in my body has been sucked out. I want to see her; I desperately want to see her; my chest is burning. Tears well up in my eyes. The pain is enough to make them spill over, though whether they're born of sadness or frustration, I couldn't say.

And then I think something.

"I won't let her."

I won't let her leave me.

I will track down Maria, no matter what I have to do. *No matter what I have to do. If I have to kill everyone in the world, then I will.*

I take out the bottle of peppermint-scented oil from my bag. I bought it on the way home from school. I walk around dripping it here and there on the floor. The familiar scent spreads, but it's not a relief at all. It's still not enough. Leaving a few drops won't be enough for the smell to wash over me.

Just…let…me…breathe.

"Haah…ah, haah!"

Maria.

The original Maria, before she obtained a Box. The Maria she's never let me see, new and untouched.

—The zeroth Maria.

Where are you?

If you are inside Aya Otonashi, then I'll pull you out, even if I have to tear off her skin.

—Click.

Out of nowhere comes the sound of the door opening.

I panic. I don't need to say I'm trespassing. I'm even putting down scented oil as if I own the place. If it's someone from the company that manages these apartments, I'm in big trouble.

But I realize my worries are unfounded when I see who appears behind the door.

No, I wasn't nearly worried enough.

The situation just got even worse.

It can't get any worse, in fact.

"O."

She presents herself in the form of the woman who somehow resembles Maria.

We've run into each other several times. We've even had relatively mundane encounters that weren't connected to anything major. This time, the implications are different from before.

O has unmistakably arrived here as my enemy.

She is here to take me down.

"Have you made your preparations?" she asks with her characteristic creepy smile.

—*For what?*

I ask for clarification, and O obliges.

"To say your good-byes to this world."

◆◆◆ Daiya Oomine 09/24 THU 10:45 AM ◆◆◆

I may have lost Crime, Punishment, and the Shadow of Crime, but I haven't forgotten anything about Boxes. I don't know the reason, but I think it may have something to do with how I knew they existed even before I got one of my own.

I walk the streets of Shinjuku. It's crowded. The number of people is annoying, but it doesn't make me dizzy anymore. I don't see any crimes when I step on shadows. I know that the sludge-like corruption lurks beneath the skin of the people strolling the packed sidewalks, but they don't appear to me like squirming bags of filth.

They're just people.

I try to brush my earrings, then remember I don't have anything in my ear and smile ruefully.

I suddenly drop to my knees in the middle of the street. I stretch my back and give a snappy bow with my head to the ground, like a karate student to a teacher.

It's a weird thing to do, from anyone's point of view.

Okay.

I raise my head. While there are several people giving me odd looks, for the most part everyone simply passes me by and tries not to get involved. That's all that happens when I'm the only one acting strangely. That's all I am now that I've lost the ability to manipulate the masses.

I don't have the power to make anything happen anymore.

"......Heh-heh."

I'm fine with that.

The people flow by without interacting with me.

Yeah, that's how it is.

The world has become a group of people who have nothing to do with me.

It's incredibly freeing.

But—

Someone suddenly taps me on the shoulder as I wade through the throngs.

I turn around, wondering who it could be.

"Oh, it's you."

When I see who it is, my expression turns tense. To be honest, it's someone I had hoped not to see.

"What could you possibly want from me now?"

Her eyes go wide at my rather rude reply, and she makes a desperate appeal. She's so worked up and all over the place, I can hardly make heads or tails of what she's saying. Listening patiently, I finally get the gist of it: She wants me to behave like a god again and set the world straight.

"You want me to lead you again? You know that's not going to happen. I don't have power anymore... You don't care? Sorry, I don't get that... Okay, let me say it loud and clear. I have no desire to do anything of the sort ever again, and I have no intention of doing it, either."

That doesn't satisfy her, though. She's still fervently pleading with me. Pretty persistent for someone with no memory of the Box.

"Responsibility? Yeah, sure. I plan on turning myself in once Kokone's condition stabilizes. Killing Koudai Kamiuchi isn't a crime I can just sweep aside, after all... What? That's not what you're talking about? Okay, then what do you mean by responsibility? ...My responsibility for leading you? I'm telling you—you're free to go. Isn't that enough? ......Huh? That's not true at all. Your life does not belong to me. It never has. It's always been yours, not mine."

Not even that gets her to back off.

"Give me a break here. Don't expect anything else from me. I'm just a high schooler—heck, I'm not even that. I'm just a failure of a person who couldn't even handle high school. Yeah. I'm human."

She persists with her desperate entreaty.

Guide me, she begs, *help me.*

What does she want from me?

I turn my back, realizing that any further conversation is pointless.

"Live however you want from now on."

I won't have anything to do with her ever again.

On that point, I've made my intentions clear.

I have completely renounced every last bit of my former power.

Then my back is hot, almost burning.

"Huh?"

My strength suddenly gives out, and I drop to my knees.

As my knees hit the ground, the blood draining out of me stains them red.

Spitting blood from my mouth, I look up at the one who stabbed me, and I realize. I'd been talking with this girl for a bit now, but I hadn't recognized her at all. Talking with her was like talking with a virtual image.

Now that it's come to this, I can finally take in what she looks like.

She had to stab me to make me acknowledge her existence.

"You're human? Please don't treat me like I'm stupid." This girl with empty eyes stands over me and says, "You are a god."

This middle schooler with a bob lowers a large kitchen knife. She rubs the blood over her face like makeup.

"If you aren't a god, then how am I supposed to live? You should be held accountable. You should be held accountable until the very end."

Screams arise from the busy thoroughfare as people notice what is happening.

"I won't let you."

She smiles through her welling tears.

"I won't let you be human again."

With that, the girl runs off, bumping into several people along the crowded street.

Before long, I can't even see her back anymore. But I'm sure the guilt of what she's done will track her down in no time. She'll come up against an overwhelming impasse. The kind world, the just world, will not protect her. That's how our world is.

I might have tried to play at being a god, but I couldn't guide anyone in the right way. This is what it gets me.

"———Ha."

Blood spills out of my mouth again.

"———Ha-ha."

This is my reward for my efforts, isn't it? Pitiful. I can't help a wry laugh.

But when I give it some thought, this really is what I get. Why did I think I should feel so free without undergoing any sort of punishment? Did I really believe the things I had done would go away completely?

Even without my powers, I'm still attacking and under attack.

This is reaping what I've sown. I had always imagined my eventual downfall. In a sense, this is just the arrival of a conclusion I foresaw for myself.

And yet.

Knowing that I brought this on myself doesn't change anything.

"……Don't…make me…laugh."

I'm filled with regret.

I don't want to be destroyed anymore. I don't want to meet this end. Those desires are gone now, yet this is my end just because I once set the wheels in motion?

There was never any going back for me? …Shut up. What am I supposed to do? I can't believe how much—

"………I…don't want…to die."

The blood trickling from my mouth makes the words almost inaudible. I'm in pain. It hurts. It hurts. I'm in so much pain.

I want to live.

Kokone.

Kokone, I want to see you.

Once blind, I've finally seen the light and come to understand the truth. I don't need to do anything. I could even be a burden. I just want to stay by your side. I've realized that's what I want, and what I have to do… And now, even after this revelation…

My wish will be crushed just like that?

Don't be stupid.

Fighting back the pain, I rise unsteadily to my feet.

I can't let myself lose so easily. I can't die. There should be a police box nearby. I'll try to make it there.

No one on those busy streets offers to help the bleeding boy. Each and every one of them simply steers clear of me without trying to help. Everyone remains as apathetic as ever in the world I couldn't change.

Is this something else I'm reaping for my trouble?

I try to laugh, but I can't. Simply put, I'm at the end of my rope. My legs are turning to jelly. My consciousness is fading away. The world is spinning.

Then it ends.

I collapse in a pathetic, motionless heap.

Something occurs to me.

If there was someone to help me out of this, they would be the definition of hope.

That's what I think.

"Are you okay, Oomine?!"

I pick him up and cradle him.

"......Aya?"

He whispers one word, then closes his eyes.

My gray jacket is stained a dark red in no time at all. His wound is worse than Kirino's was, and unlike back then, I don't have any first aid implements.

Before long, I know I can't save him.

It's no coincidence that I was able to hurry to Daiya in his moment of need. With nowhere else to go, I had been following him. It didn't mean anything more than that. Oomine had once given me the opportunity to do away with the "misbegotten" part of my Misbegotten Happiness, so I'd been trailing him in the hope that maybe I would find the same chance again. Chances were slim to none, but I couldn't give up.

When Oomine faintly gasps "You really did come" with faint breaths, I get the impression that maybe he knew what I was doing.

But I doubt that's the case. Oomine once attempted to entrust his power to me. I may have lost Crime, Punishment, and the Shadow of Crime, but I believe I still embody hope for him.

I'm honored, but it hurts to know I won't be able to live up to his expectations.

"Hold on, I'll call an ambulance. You have to try and stay conscious until then." I offer him something, knowing it may be no use. He opens and closes his mouth, enduring the pain.

"Use......on me."

"What? What're you trying to say?"

Summoning the last of his strength, he tells me what he wants—the one method that could save him.

"Use the Misbegotten Happiness on me."

Erasing my memories of Kazuki Hoshino.

That's what using the Misbegotten Happiness on Oomine would mean.

No, I'm not okay with the idea. That hasn't changed, even if he has. I spent a whole lifetime with him; he has power over my heart no matter what I have to say about it. —And power is what it is. Kazuki haunts all the more human portions of my heart. He's scattered everywhere, so I can't be rid of him.

If I forget Kazu, I won't be myself anymore. I'd become a sort of doppelgänger of myself, just with the same body and purpose.

Discarding myself.

That is terrifying.

I can't believe this... How did I neglect this problem until it came to this? Why didn't I get away from Kazuki from the beginning?

Was I lazy, relaxing into the comfort of his presence? Was I enjoying life at the expense of my mission?

No.

I shake my head internally. My connection with Kazuki is not so frail. It wasn't something I could overcome by just holding on to the right attitude. This may be a strange way of putting it, but my deepening ties to him were unavoidable. There is nothing that could have been done as long as the Rejecting Classroom existed.

I accept it.

The bond between Kazuki and me is absolute.

It's a precious connection born of necessity.

And now I will destroy it.

"_____!"

...Don't be afraid, I've said so many times.

But if that's true—

—I can't help but wonder.

Is there any meaning to the "me" who vanishes over and over? She's destined to be lost—so can you say she really exists?

What am "I"?

But the me who is thinking about these things is suddenly amused.

"......Heh-heh."

What's the point of going over all this with myself now?

"I"—am a Box.

A Box with no meaning beyond granting the wishes of others.

And here, right before my eyes, is someone who wishes for the Misbegotten Happiness.

I smile at Oomine.

"Okay, I'll use the Misbegotten Happiness."

No hesitation. I'm a Box; I shouldn't have doubts.

"Please."

Oomine reaches out with a blood-drenched hand for my cheek. The weak touch of his fingers tells me that this is nearly it for him.

"I don't want to die."

A thought suddenly comes to me.

There was once a girl trapped within a looping world who had a similar wish. She couldn't fully believe she wouldn't die, and that was the result.

Oomine is a realist, so I'm sure he won't be able to ignore his own fate.

Meaning that even if I do use the Misbegotten Happiness, the outcome will be—

I decide not to entertain that thought any further.

If someone asks to be saved, then my only course is to meet that request.

I press Oomine's bloody hand against my chest.

And then I—disappear.

Disappear.

Disappear.

I sink to the bottom of the ocean. It's pitch-black there, and I can't see a thing. Not even my own hands. I can't even be sure of my own form. It's cold, and my body turns numb as it freezes over. I can't tell where I am. I may be the oceanic abyss itself.

I can hear distant laughter. Lots of laughing voices. They don't have anything to do with me, though. Plus, their joy is fake.

No one can see themselves here, so there's no need for pretense. The water pressure has pressed out the softer parts of me, leaving me in a state I can never let anyone else see. It's my weak self. The girl I used to be. But there's no one here anyway, so it doesn't really matter.

The world is far away.

I am farther away than anyone.

But an unexpected light appears to me in my solitude. It's harsh and intense, like a spotlight catching a criminal. My eyes narrow against the glare.

Then she reveals herself.

I say the name of the girl who appears.

"O."

I notice something immediately, though.

She's different. No, she is undoubtedly O, but not the same. This form of hers. This girl with the bewitching smile, she's—

"Aya...my sister."

And then my eyes are opened.

How my Box works. How the Misbegotten Happiness remains a failure. How my own actions serve no purpose. How everything I've done until now was just swimming around lost in the pitch-black ocean depths. How my memories have left me ignorant.

I understand everything.

So what about me? What have I been doing all this for?

"Maria." *She says my name.* "You remember my wish, right?"

"Of course I do."

It's the only way I can atone.

The one thing I can do for my beloved sister.

There was something Aya always used to say, and she says it again now. "I want to make other people happy."

"Okay." *All I can do is nod in agreement.*

"Will you keep making my wish come true?"

"Yes," *I reply, and Aya answers with a charming smile.*

Overjoyed, I try to smile along with her. My head is frozen, though, so I can't tell if I'm really succeeding.

"As you do, you will probably keep wandering. What is flawed and incomplete will remain flawed, but you will never stop pursuing perfection. You will continue to forget yourself in your search for a correct answer that doesn't exist."

"Maybe so…"

"But that's what you wanted."

"What do you mean? What I wanted?"

"To continually seek out the ideal—that is your wish." She smiles. I always loved that smile. "If you become whole, then you will realize that Aya Otonashi doesn't exist within you."

"Oh, I see."

So what I'm doing, really, is—

"————Anyway."

I do know one thing.

I won't stop, even though what I do may be meaningless in the end, as meaningless as swimming around down here in the depths of the sea.

That's right; I—

"There's no one who can stop me."

I then come to my senses. I'm sitting on my knees in the middle of a busy street in Shinjuku. My posture suggests I have been holding someone, but there's no one in my arms.

I glance down and see that I'm covered in blood. I don't know why. Surprisingly, I'm not shocked or frightened.

I don't remember anything. But I do know what happened to me.

I used the Misbegotten Happiness.

There's a gulf in my head. It's vast, too large to fill in. A pit so massive that I might start shaking if I look directly at it.

Yes, I have lost it.

Once again, I've become something other than myself.

I rise unsteadily to my feet. My body feels strangely light, causing me to stagger. I see myself reflected in a shop window. My face looks awful, as if I'm bearing the misery of the whole world, and I'm so gaunt that I appear completely helpless. I guess this is what I amount to when I forget my resolve.

Deciding to go somewhere else, I realize I have no place to go.

With no memories of my family, no memories of my friends, I have no mooring.

As I stand completely still, a busy-looking man who seems like an office worker bumps into me. He glances at me when I stagger, and he clicks his tongue, then quickly hurries off.

—Where am I?

—Who am I?

I feel as if I'm at the very bottom of the ocean.

"   "

I suddenly get the feeling someone is calling out to me.

The way they address me brings warmth to my heart. It's so familiar. For a moment, it feels as though asking who it is would be a ridiculous thing to do.

I turn around.

But the people on the street are paying no attention to me, so there doesn't seem to be anyone who would have called out to me like that.

"   "

There it is again.

A voice that moves my heart.

But I realize something. While I feel as if I can hear the voice, I can't tell what it's saying.

"What...?" I touch my cheek. "Why am I crying?"

I don't understand.

I'm sure, though, that whatever this is was important to the girl I once was.

It has nothing to do with me anymore, but maybe it was something I shouldn't have lost.

Yes, but still.

It doesn't matter to me anymore.

I wipe away my tears. No more come to replace them.

I haven't forgotten my purpose. Granting the wishes of other people—that is what's important to me. Nothing else. I have to put aside what my former self once cherished.

No, I already have.

Now then, it's time to find O again.

"......Huh?"

What did I just think?

I try to pull it back, but nothing comes to me. I can't recall what I was thinking just now. I get the feeling it doesn't really matter, though.

I will keep wandering, and that's all.

And so I forget O's true nature yet again.

AFTERWORD

Hello, Eiji Mikage here.

I have delivered to you the sixth volume of *The Empty Box and Zeroth Maria*. The events of the final stages of this story are things I have envisioned in my head for quite some time now, so it is all the more moving to be able to put them to paper.

This may seem a bit out of the blue, but my motto is "A pro cannot be human."

It comes from a statement spoken on TV by Oh, a coach of the Hawks at the time whom I admired. My memory of them may be a little off, but here is the gist of what he said:

"All humans make mistakes. But an athlete who thinks they can't do anything about their mistakes because they are human will make the same errors again. Thus, a pro cannot be human."

I remember being deeply impressed, thinking that having such a strong sense of what it is to be a professional must be what enabled him to hammer out the record he did.

Regardless of whether you're a pro baseball player or not, I feel that a high level of awareness that verges on going beyond what is human is necessary in adhering to a singular will. I'm nowhere near that level yet, but I'm working hard to try to get there someday.

Now for my acknowledgements.

To my editor, Miki: Thank you very much for keeping things going smoothly amid your exceedingly busy schedule.

To my illustrator, Tetsuo: Thank you for the wonderful art as always. I look forward to seeing your illustrations every time and consider it to be a part of why I'm writing this story.

*   *   *

Welp, there is only one more installment left in the tale. When I think about it, this has been an undertaking that has proved so difficult, it almost makes me cry uncle each time I turn in another volume. I've made it here at last. I swear that I will write out the story to the end, so I hope you'll come along for the ride.

I will also be unveiling a new project come springtime. I have the feeling that readers of this story will enjoy it, too, so I hope you will give it a look.

I'm pouring my heart into both of them, so please don't go saying *Hurry up and get the last book out!* okay?

Have faith that we'll see each other again.

Eiji Mikage